W9-BLO-821

# Arizona
# Dreams

# Arizona
# Dreams

## Jon Talton

Poisoned Pen Press

Poisoned Pen Press
6962 E. First Ave., Ste. 103
Scottsdale, AZ 85251
www.poisonedpenpress.com
info@poisonedpenpress.com

Printed in the United States of America

*For Susan*

# Acknowledgments

Paying my debts: My deepest thanks go to Barbara Peters and Robert Rosenwald at the Poisoned Pen Press.

Also, I'm indebted to my Arizona friends Linda Weaver, Jim Ballinger and Randy Edmond. May all their Arizona dreams come true.

# Chapter One

I knew what was coming. A gentleman reaches a point in his life when he knows the moment a woman wants to be kissed. He knows the moment when she has decided to kiss him. I acquired this critical intuition in my early thirties—probably later than most, but I had spent more time in libraries than on dates when I was younger. Although I had seemed to start kissing with promise, at fourteen, when a girl named Wendy planted a revelation on me. "Close your eyes," she ordered. Wendy was a younger woman of thirteen, but she knew things, as girls always do.

Now I knew and I could see what was coming. Even so, I'm not sure I could teach it the way I once could breeze through a semester of lectures about American history. How do you know that moment? It's something in the eyes, a widening and darkening perhaps. It's an expectant upward tilt of the head, especially if the woman is standing close. She was sitting across from me, but I could still sense that tilt. Around us, Portland's bar was busy for July in Phoenix, a brutal month of a brutal season. The let-me-die-in-peace season of my hometown, when the rich flee for cooler climes and even triumphs seem freighted with sweaty hopelessness. "Never make life decisions in the summer," was one of Lindsey's axioms. The area around the bar was bright with conversation, and through the large windows I could see a dust storm was boiling. I had had to speak loudly to make myself heard, and she had talked, too. Then there seemed to be nothing more to say. And that's when she raised up, leaned over and brought her lips to mine.

When a man is really crazy about a woman, he will inevitably begin to talk like a teenage boy cataloging his pinup fantasy. So let me admit my bias about Lindsey up front. These are the facts: She stands five feet seven inches, and although she won't tell me her weight, she seems average. She has fair skin that doesn't tan. Her hair is a very dark brown, just one shade above black, naturally straight. Lately she had been wearing it shorter, in a pageboy with bangs. Her eyes are dark blue, and her lashes are unremarkable. Little crinkles have begun to appear around her eyes, just as the lines around her mouth have deepened. But those only come out when she smiles, a wondrous event. It's her mouth that men probably first notice and they would call it "sensual." That, and her legs, which she would say are her best physical features. She is the kindest and wisest person I know.

I could tell you more, but it would just be my opinion. What I did know for sure was that my eyes were still open at that moment, and I saw Lindsey standing just outside the bar, watching this kiss. Even if I had been of a mind to run after her, she was gone by the next time I looked in that direction.

How we all reached that moment, I couldn't exactly say. But I knew when it began. It began, like too much of my recent history, with a killing.

# Chapter Two

The Willo Historic District is a mile long and half a mile wide. Every February, it holds a home tour that attracts thousands of people to its narrow, palm-lined streets and Period Revival and bungalow houses built in the early decades of the last century. That year, as usual, Lindsey and I made Bloody Marys and sat on the front patio, in preparation for watching the people streaming down Cypress Street past our 1924 Spanish Colonial house.

Our house wasn't on the tour, and I suspected it never would be. Lindsey didn't want a few thousand people tromping through her living room. And our Sheriff's Department salaries didn't allow us to do the big rehab jobs that had gone on up and down the street. The neighborhood had changed since I had grown up in the house, then gone off to college and spent many years away from Phoenix. When I was a kid, it was headed down on its heels. People didn't want to live close to downtown in old houses. But tastes change, and today Willo was one of the more expensive neighborhoods outside of Paradise Valley and North Scottsdale. Many of the houses had been lovingly restored and enhanced, and now the neighborhood held the mix of gays and dual-income-no-kids straights you find anywhere in urban America, plus a few families with children. There was a handful of old families that remembered me, plus a few eccentrics and cranks.

We settled into our chairs a little before ten a.m., starting time for the home tour, to enjoy the people watching and the Sunday newspapers. Lindsey had mapped out three houses she wanted to see later, if the lines to get in weren't too long. Above us, the sky was a magnificent deep blue with a few scattered fat white clouds. The temperature was on the warm side of seventy-five. It was the kind of day that seemed all magic and promise, with the hell of summer just a memory.

"You're in the paper, Dave."

Lindsey was reading the *Arizona Republic*. I looked at her over the first section of *The New York Times*.

"I didn't realize you were a 'liberal elite academic seeking to undermine traditional American values,'" she said. "Although, you've done your part to lead me astray, and I've enjoyed every minute of it."

"Give me that." I took the paper and read:

> Maricopa County Supervisor Tom Earley on Saturday blasted the Sheriff's Office for spending money on such items as a historian to work cold cases and for failing to address what he called the greatest problem facing Arizona, illegal immigration.
>
> Speaking at Golden Sunrise Church in Chandler, Earley took special aim at Deputy David Mapstone, a former professor who has solved several notorious cases from Phoenix's past.
>
> "Professors like Mapstone are liberal elite academics seeking to undermine traditional American values, and your tax dollars are paying for it," Earley said to sustained applause. "Mapstone only has this job because he's a friend of Sheriff Peralta. So what you have here is cronyism on top of a terrible waste of taxpayers' money and just plain ridiculousness. What does some history professor know about anything?"

I handed the paper back and sipped the Bloody Mary, wishing I had upped the vodka. "Sustained applause?"

"It's the East Valley," she sighed. "The reddest red state is too blue for them."

"I'm surprised Peralta hasn't called."

"Dave," Lindsey said, smiling, "this ridiculousness must stop."

I was about to take a deep gulp when a man came running up our walk.

"You got to come," he panted, standing bent over, his hands on his knees.

"What's up, Jim?" I only knew him by his first name, a man from somewhere in the neighborhood who walked a big dog early in the morning and sometimes stopped to talk.

"We need help," he said. "There's a man...I think he might be dead..."

"Where?" Lindsey asked. He gave a street number, a block away, and we rose and followed him. We moved at a quick trot west on Cypress, stepping out into the street to get around the tour-goers. Fire Station Four was five blocks away and the neighborhood had its share of current and retired cops. But there we were on our porch, and a neighbor was asking for help. We crossed Fifth Avenue and up ahead I could see a disorganized crowd gathered on the sidewalk, all turning to watch us.

We slowed to a walk and people let us through. Ahead was a two-story Monterey revival house with a perfect lawn and perfect citrus trees out front. It was the most impressive place on the block, with a long balcony and ornate railing. Its door was standing open. Jim was talking as we went up the sidewalk.

"This house was supposed to be on the tour," he said, wiping sweat from his forehead. "But when the committee came by this morning to help get ready, nobody answered and the door was standing open..."

By that time, we were inside.

"It's down this hall," he said.

Somebody had spent a sweet inheritance on the place. Off the entryway was a living room that looked straight out of *Architectural*

*Digest:* dark, Mission-style furniture, flawless barrel ceiling, ornate Spanish tile around the fireplace, and Indian pottery of a size and quality I usually saw only at the Heard Museum. There were the remains of a fire in the fireplace, but I didn't have time to linger.

"Here," Jim said, standing before a doorway.

I stepped into a bedroom, followed by Lindsey. It was probably a nice bedroom, with a sweet smell in the air and French doors looking out on a shaded courtyard, but I felt like an intruder. A man was asleep in the middle of a king-size bed. He was a tall, dark-haired man, lying naked atop the covers. But then my eye went to the right side of his head and I knew he wasn't sleeping. A handle was attached to the man's ear.

"What is that thing, Dave?" Lindsey spoke softly.

I said, "It's an ice pick."

We both turned to Jim.

"Who else lives here?" Lindsey asked.

Jim shook his head. "A lawyer, I think. He lived alone…

"I didn't let anybody come in, once I found him," he stammered. He was still sweating profusely.

I walked carefully around to one side of the bed. Before I got to the carotid pulse I could tell he was dead. His skin had that corpse coldness that you never forget once you've touched it.

I knew everybody in my block of Cypress, but I didn't know this one. And even if I might recognize the man in the bed, that would have to wait for the detectives and evidence techs. His face was hidden, buried in a pillow, and all I saw was a nice haircut and a misplaced kitchen tool.

"OK." I took a deep breath. "Let's go over to your house and use the phone." But as I looked over at Lindsey, I saw my ever-resourceful wife had brought her cell phone and was using it.

Later, after the city cops were through with us, we started back home. The tour organizers were expecting fifteen thousand people, and out on the sidewalk it seemed as if a few hundred were watching our show, along with an obligatory TV news crew. I bet this would have been the best house they'd see, if they could have gotten inside. And they would have received the bonus of seeing how one human being could drive an ice pick into another human being's brain, neat as can be. I suppressed an involuntary shiver as Lindsey took my hand.

We crouched to get under the yellow tape. Then, the people on the sidewalk made way for us. Nobody talked. And that's when I saw her. Most everybody was watching the house, and the official comings and goings. But she was watching me. At first, I might have mistaken her for a man: a young, cute man. The kind of boy who makes teenaged girls melt. She was wearing a loose, sleeveless T-shirt, the kind you see at a gym, and cargo shorts that reached to her knees, and something about her was tough looking. Her arms were muscled, and her face was what a less politically correct age would call mannish. Her hair was straw blond, carelessly pushed back under a newsboy's cap turned backward. But her calves were shapely and smooth—a small tattoo that looked like a Chinese character decorated one ankle—and I detected breasts pushing against the T-shirt. This was an interesting, striking, androgynous person, and I needed something to take my mind off death on a Sunday morning.

"Lindsey."

We stopped and turned, and it was the same woman. She had not quite a smile on her face.

"Hey, Lindsey," she said again. "You're a real cop now…"

Lindsey was still wearing her badge, on a chain around her neck. Her hand stiffened in mine, and then pulled away.

"Hello, Robin. What are you doing here?"

"I live near here. I just got back to Phoenix this winter. Are you here for the tour?"

Lindsey said nothing.

The woman stood there smiling. It brought all her features together, and her face was suddenly more attractive. She looked me over and smiled more.

"So are you going to introduce me to your friend?"

Lindsey bit her lip, then said, "This is my husband, David Mapstone. Dave, this is my sister, Robin."

# Chapter Three

"I didn't know Lindsey had a sister," Peralta said.

"Nor did I."

"'Nor did I.' You talk weird, Mapstone. Like some college professor. No wonder Tom Earley doesn't like you." He didn't smile. He inclined his head to one side, as if a weight had attached itself to his ear. "Is she good looking?"

I stared at him.

"No," I said. "Well, maybe. I don't know. Jeez, she's my sister-in-law." The words still sounded strange. The lost sister that I'd never heard of. Robin and Lindsey. Our encounter lasted all of five minutes. No sisterly embrace. No invitation back to our house. I had never seen Lindsey so uncomfortable, or, later that evening, so quietly withdrawn.

"What does she do for a living?" Peralta demanded.

"She says she's an art curator."

"You mean like in a museum?"

"No," I said. "For some rich person out in Paradise Valley. And, no, I didn't know there were jobs like that, either."

Peralta made a dissatisfied grunt. I knew what he meant. We were sitting in my office on the fourth floor of the old county courthouse. Behind the county-issue nameplate that read DEPUTY DAVID MAPSTONE, SHERIFF'S OFFICE HISTORIAN. I was behind the old walnut desk. But he had his feet on it, propped from the straight-back chair in front, in a proprietary way. My desktop was hosting highly polished black cowboy boots, attached to a big man in a dark suit. He still had a full head of hair, and it was as lustrously black as the first day I met him, so many years before. He was one of those men who grew handsome as they aged, and his face was distinguished with strong cheekbones, a powerful jaw and large black eyes that could intimidate with a half-second glance.

He went on. "So did you meet her before or after the murder?"

I told him the timetable.

"Ice pick, huh," he said, his fingers entwining across his big chest. "I bet it was a fruit salad thing."

"Fruit salad?"

"Sure," he said, making an obscene gesture. "Lover's spat that got out of hand. Maybe some new sex toy experiment."

"You are such an automatic reactionary," I said. "I dare you to say those things to your voters. What have I said that makes you think gay?"

"Man living alone in the Willo District. A lawyer, no less. In bed. Strange device. What more do I need to say?" He glared at me smugly.

"I'm not gay, and Lindsey's not gay, and we live in Willo. It's a city neighborhood with diversity and tolerance. Unlike your mansion on the Phoenix Mountain Preserve."

"'Reactionary.' 'Diversity.' You sound like my ex-wife." His eyes refused to meet mine.

I didn't let the silence gather. "You might be interested to know that an ice pick into the brain was one of the methods used by Murder Inc. You know, the organized crime outfit back in the 1950s?"

"That's why I pay you, Mapstone. For all the history lessons." He gave an exaggerated yawn.

"Of course, Murder Inc. took the ice pick with them. The idea was to make it look like a cerebral hemorrhage," I said halfway to myself. "This one was done so we'd see it and pay attention. Nothing appeared to be taken. The house wasn't in disarray, no sign of a fight or struggle. The door was standing open. The alarm had not been tripped."

"That makes my point," the sheriff said, leaning back farther in the chair, daring gravity.

"Might be a psycho killer."

"You watch too much TV," he said. "Actually, you don't watch TV—that's your problem. Look, it's a gay thing, and you know it." His eyes locked onto mine. "Now, don't go being a nosy neighbor or acting like a hotdog rookie. This is a city case and you have plenty to do here. How is our book coming?"

"Our" book was supposed to be about the big cases I'd worked on since coming back to Phoenix and taking the job at the Sheriff's Department. My odd personal history consisted of five years as a deputy sheriff, much of it as Peralta's partner, then 15 years as a college history professor. Back with a badge, I worked on the old unsolved cases, using a historian's techniques to budge them, if not solve them. It had turned into a little media bonanza for the sheriff. Now he wanted the most notorious cases we had solved compiled in a book. For which he, of course, would write the introduction.

"I'm getting to it…" I started.

"Getting to it?" Peralta said. He pulled down his legs and sat up straight.

"I've got other work." I pointed to a pile of manila folders on the desktop. "You wanted me to go back and look at the 1976 Don Bolles case, remember?"

"That can wait," he said.

"I'm supposed to start teaching at ASU this fall, a course on urban American history. I need to prepare for that. It's just one course, but it will be nice to be back on a campus again."

"Why do I care?"

"Because you want me to be happy?" He frowned. "I didn't think so. It will be good publicity for you. And I've been contacted by a bank in Chicago—this is kind of cool. They want me to research whether one of the banks they bought in Louisiana was ever connected to slavery."

"Quit fucking around!" he barked, his voice deepening with finality. He smoothed his thick hair back and pointed a meaty finger at me. "There's an election coming up, and don't assume the next sheriff will need a history professor."

"You'll be sheriff until you decide to become governor," I shot back. "And I serve at your pleasure, if such a thing is possible. If you didn't want me to stay, why did you try to talk me out of the job at Portland State?"

"You didn't get it anyway," he said. "You don't have enough of that precious diversity you talk about." His eyes narrowed smugly. "I was defending you the other day against the county supervisors."

"Me, personally?"

He nodded. "They were questioning your salary. Why pay it when DNA and forensic evidence is the way other counties are clearing cases today. They also didn't like keeping your office here after the building was rehabbed."

I watched his face for a hint that he was joking: a slight lift in his eyebrow, an extra watt in the eyes. His expression was impassive. My stomach was suddenly hurting. Our conversation had gone from idle to nasty in racecar time.

"I thought that nut Earley was just grandstanding."

"That nut represents a lot of voters," Peralta said, leaning forward and sketching something indecipherable on my desk.

I said, "So he wants to cut funding for public schools and Child Protective Services, then decry why we have so many young people who end up in your jail."

"That may be true," Peralta said, "but it doesn't seem to matter when people vote. They respond to this stuff that Earley says. He's the face of the new Republican Party, Mapstone, and you'd better believe they want to knock me off in the primary. And I mean as sheriff. Forget about governor."

"That's ridiculous. You're an institution. A legend."

He grunted and shook his head. "Times change, and in their eyes I'm just somebody with brown skin." I looked at him. Peralta was incapable of irony.

"This town runs on two engines," he said, "conservative politics and real estate. And Tom Earley is big in both. He made a fortune developing shopping centers. He's incredibly connected. He's ambitious as hell…"

"So what do you want me to do?" I asked, my voice rising. "Give him a campaign contribution? Resign?"

"If you lose your job, you can sell that house," he said. "Have you seen the price appreciation for those old houses? I don't get it. But, hell, you could sell it, buy a bunch of rental houses, leverage the hell out of your equity…"

"Thanks for the vote of confidence," I said.

He sniffed and cleared his throat. "The main reason I tried to talk you out of going to Portland was your wife. I couldn't lose Lindsey. She's my star. She's one of the top computer crime experts in the country now, Mapstone. She works with the feds as often as she works for me. She means a half-million-dollar grant from the feds to the Sheriff's Office. I'd have had to make her divorce you if you went to Oregon…" He sat back and drummed his big fingers on his belly. "Do you get my point? These guys like Earley are gunning for me and for you. So if you want to keep playing cop and playing historian, you'd better…"

"I'll write the goddamned book," I snarled. "So you can run for governor."

He was about to say something when a knock came at the office door.

"Dr. Mapstone?" The voice went to a woman, who leaned her head around the door. I beckoned her in. Peralta stood and strode out with the grace that only certain big men can manage.

# Chapter Four

"Was that Mike Peralta, the sheriff?" the woman asked.

"No," I said. "It was Mike Peralta, the asshole. They're often mistaken for one another."

She looked at me wide-eyed, and then filled the room with laughter. A nice laugh.

"You haven't changed a bit." She shook her head fondly and sat in one of the straight-backed chairs. "You're also just as tall, dark, and handsome as I remember."

Pleasant-looking, you'd call her. In glasses, with tortoise-shell rims. Maybe around thirty-five, with strawberry-blond hair, parted on one side and falling to her shoulders. Dressed in a copper-colored sweater and navy skirt. The sweater made her pinkish skin seem more flushed. It was a pleasantly forgettable face. You'd have to spend a lot of time with that face to find it remarkable. I had no idea who she was.

"Miss…?"

"Oh, I'm sorry." She stood hastily and thrust her hand across the desk. I shook it. "There's no reason you should know me. I was one of your students, Dana Underwood. I was Dana Watkins, then. At Miami. I guess I look different now." She smiled. Smiling, it was a better face.

I smiled back and invited her to sit down. As an itinerant history professor I had taught at Miami University in Ohio, the University of Denver, and finally San Diego State. At Miami, I was not much older than my students and teaching the kind of survey courses where the class size is not as large as the crowd at a Suns game. I must have made quite an impression for her to look me up.

"This is a beautiful old building," she said. "I didn't even know Phoenix had any old buildings."

I told her it was built in 1929.

"My gosh," she said. "They didn't even have electricity then, right?"

I couldn't tell if she was joking or not. You never knew these days. So I just smiled. If she had been one of my students, she hadn't had much aptitude for history. In a moment, she started talking again.

"My husband was transferred out here with Motorola a few years ago. He was laid off, but that's a different subject. Anyway, I started seeing your name in the papers, as the history expert who worked as a deputy. I always thought there's no history here, it's so new. But when I'd see your name, I'd say, 'I was in that guy's class.'"

"Thanks for remembering," I said. I wasn't a good listener just then. I was stuck back in Peralta World, thinking of what I should have said to him.

She said, "You were a wonderful teacher, Dr. Mapstone."

"How about David."

"David," she said, and folded her hands neatly in her lap. Her eyes were watery, making her seem on the verge of tears even when she smiled. Her eyes made a track of my office. It was not much different from when it opened in 1929, with sumptuous dark wood paneling, deco light globes, and tall multi-paned windows with curved tops. I had scavenged the furniture from county storage, and added too many books.

"I can't believe how much time has passed. I see you're married now." She pointed to my wedding band. "Do you have kids?" I said I didn't. "I have two, can you believe it? Madison is seventeen and a senior, and Noah is a junior. They're great kids. I never thought I'd be a soccer mom."

"Good for you," I said.

She cleared her throat, and started again. "I came here today because I need help." I didn't recognize her, but I recognized her voice. Even serious, it had a lilt, as if you could turn butterscotch into sound. Where did that voice fit in my past?

I thought about what Peralta had said. It wasn't like I had time to be helping former students. But I said I'd do anything I could. David Mapstone, always happy to help the taxpayers of Maricopa County and avoid sitting down to write.

Dana Underwood pulled an envelope from her purse and set it carefully on my desk. It looked unremarkable, a white No. 10 envelope. I half wondered if she was here to contest an old grade with me.

"Now, David, it takes me awhile to get to the point. This drives my husband crazy, but it's just the way I am." Her hand brushed back her hair, tucked it behind a small pale ear. One reddish strand still fell against her glasses. "You see, my father died last year. Cancer."

"I'm sorry."

"Thank you, but after he died it was up to me to go through his things. He was a pack rat, and mother was in no condition…this is all back in Rocky River. I can't say I was close to my dad. I didn't really know him. He was a self-made man. He'd started out working the ore boats out of Cleveland. And he saved enough to buy some old rental houses and fix them up. That's how he got his start. He never even graduated from high school. But he did really well in real estate, which is how he could pay to send his children to places like Miami. He even bought land out here. It's still in the family."

I put a finger on the envelope. "Is this about your father?"

"I'm sorry," she said. "I warned you. Yes. It's a letter. To me. He wrote it, and left it in the drawer by his bed. As you can see, it says, 'to be opened after my death.' When I found it, I was a little afraid." She paused and looked around the office again. "I mean, what was it going to say? You know, you get older and see something of life, and you realize that your parents…nobody's parents are saints. So I let it sit for a few days. But then one day I read it."

She reached for the envelope, lifted it toward her, then seemed to think better of it and set it back on the desk.

"David, I think he killed a man. I think, I fear, my father killed a man."

"And you didn't know about this?"

She shook her head. "If he did, he got away with it, David."

I let out a breath, too loudly. "He confesses this in the letter?"

"That's all the letter is about," she said. "It's very matter of fact. I would rather have learned that he had a mistress or that I had been adopted…"

"Why would he write it down?"

Her hair had come loose again. She swept it back and said, "I think he finally wanted me to know. After he'd been diagnosed, and knew he didn't have long. He knew I'd take charge, and I'd find it. But the crime—if it happened—was in 1966."

"Was your father the kind of man who would kill somebody?"

"I thought he was when he found my boyfriend in bed with me when I was seventeen," she said. "And I mean that. He had a bad temper. And he'd had to have been tough to make it in Cleveland. But, no, nothing like that."

"Who was this man he killed?"

"It doesn't say. Now, don't dismiss me. I know what you're thinking. He only refers to him as 'Z.' He writes that he felt he had no choice, but nobody would have believed him. But there's so little to it—just a few sentences. No sense of really why this happened, what drove him to do it. There are so many questions."

"Dana," I said, "I'm sorry to hear this. I know it's got to be a shock, coming on top of losing your father. And I'm honored you'd look me up. But I don't really see how I can be any help."

"This is what you do, David," she said, her eyes bright. "Crime and history. I remember you said that every historian's dream is to discover a letter in an attic."

"I think I probably said something like a letter from Abe Lincoln or George Washington…"

"Well, it's not that," she said primly. "But I need to know if my father really did kill a man."

I tried to watch her closely, but instead I felt the largeness of the room around us. My eyes drifted to the *Republic* on my desk, with headlines about continuing drought, a twenty-car pileup on Interstate 10 and a six-year-old boy found chained by his parents in a box. So much trouble in my city. I said, "Do you really want to know? Sometimes it's better not to know everything."

"Yes," she said quietly. "I have to know. Wouldn't you want to know if your father was a murderer?" She pushed the envelope at me. I didn't touch it. She said, "Anyway, that's not all. The other thing he writes is where we can find the body."

I felt relief. "Then it's clear. If you really fear that this is possible, you've got to go to the police back in Ohio."

She shook her head violently, unleashing a small cascade of hair. "No, David. I came to the right police. The man is buried right here in Arizona."

# Chapter Five

A few days later, I checked out a Ford Crown Vic from the sheriff's motor pool. Lately I'd been riding the bus in anticipation of Phoenix finally finishing the light-rail line on Central; when that happened, I could take the train the mile-and-a-half between the house and my office in the old courthouse. With this well-used piece of county property, I drove west and left the city. I tried to leave the city, but it kept spreading out. The cotton and alfalfa fields that stood when I was a kid had long since been covered with subdivisions. Now many of them, once new safe suburbia, had become slums. The little farm towns had turned into cities, densely packed red tile rooftops stretching to the horizon. Farther out, the remnants of farms sat like an unwanted tenant as the shopping strips, car dealerships and houses encroached. Signs hawked new developments from a dozen builders. A billboard half the size of a football field and as well constructed as a city hall promised yet another project, the words standing out in ten-foot gossamer, "Arizona Dreams."

Where Interstate 10 curved around the booming suburb of Goodyear, the horizon opened up. The White Tank Mountains spread out in front of me, a vast purplish expanse slathered with the distinctive pale rocks that give them their odd name. The mountains, which I usually saw as a smudge to the west, suddenly looked majestic and wild. Behind them, the sky was an electric blue, ornamented with similarly bright fluffy white clouds. It was a scene increasingly rare in my town, with its dirty air. But the land I passed through was not empty. The sun glinted off the rooftops. Elsewhere, every empty parcel of land had a sign that proclaimed "available."

As traffic lightened up, I let myself hear Lindsey's voice in my head. She had awakened me at three that morning to hear the rain. It was a rare and lovely sound in the thirsty land. I slipped out from the covers to watch the drops fall with increasing force on the dark street outside. Then I came back to bed and she had warmed me. Then our hands conjured their usual magic, but later, as she lay panting, sprawled atop me, I knew her mind was someplace else.

After she had tucked her toes under my legs, as was her custom, I ventured, "Are you okay?" She just pressed her head against my shoulder and said nothing. The rain had settled into a gentle brushing sound on the roof. I listened for a while, then whispered, "Is it Robin?" But again, she had been silent, and she became so still that I thought she was asleep. I just held her, feeling her heart beat against mine.

"I spent so many years trying to escape it, Dave." She spoke in a whisper, as if she didn't want the room to hear. "Why is Robin here? Why was she on our street?"

I just listened and stroked her soft hair. Knowing that Lindsey had a tough childhood didn't help me understand her reaction to this mystery sister. I knew other things might have been on her mind, too. She was indeed the valuable one in the family, as Peralta noted. Lately she had helped bust a money-laundering operation working through a small bank in North Scottsdale. But there was nothing small about the players. The feds claimed the money was part of a complicated financing scheme involving Mexican drug lords, the Asian sex-trade, and Middle Eastern terrorists. It reminded me of the eighteenth century trade triangle of slaves, rum, and molasses. It worried Lindsey. Robin worried Lindsey. For that matter, there was an unsolved murder just down the street. There was a lot to worry us all. But it didn't seem like the right time to ask her for anything more. I could feel her tears on my skin. And then I felt her breathing smooth out, and pretty soon I was asleep, too.

Now I was so far west that the mountains had shifted. The White Tanks were to the east, and south of them the Sierra Estrella piled up massively, an unfamiliar view. Due south was a low ridge of bumpy tears in the horizon; the Gila Bend Mountains, I think. When I came off the interstate, the city was gone. After a mile of driving on a two-lane road, even the scruffy trailers and junkyards of the desert rats had been replaced by chaparral and brittlebush and empty country. The bones of an old gas station passed my window. The freeway didn't exist when Dana's father allegedly killed "Z" and buried him. The way into the desert would have been longer and more tortuous, but the directions were clear enough.

Stashing bodies in the desert was nothing new—this Harquahala Desert had been the dumping ground for a serial killer a few years back. Lindsey had finally stopped him. That had been when we were first getting together. This desert had memories, secrets. And yet another one, courtesy of a dead man's letter. I still had it locked in my desk drawer. It was one page of inexpensive white paper. The writing was in blue ink, in a jaggedy script. But it was legible, and, as she had said, it was matter-of-fact:

> Dear Dana,
>
> If you've found this letter and opened it, then I'm gone. I'm sorry to give you another shock. But it has to come out. I killed Z in March 1966. I had to. You have to know he left me no choice. I took his body out to the property west of Tonopah and buried him. It wasn't a proper burial. Just rocks.

There was one sentence in a different tone. At the bottom of the page. It read:

> Don't hate your old man, Dana. I had to do these things, for you. I loved you whether you knew it or not.

Dana didn't know who "Z"' was. All she knew was the directions to the property, which the will had made hers. Her father had a notion of raising cattle on it. But this was rough country, with little more than creosote bush covering the hard, rolling ground. Not even a Texas longhorn would last out here, which is why it was so unappealing to settlers in the nineteenth century. They passed through, if they had to, on the way to California. Yet after another thirty minutes of bumping over a dirt road, I was pretty sure I was there, and the country had changed. Several saguaros with multiple arms towered over dense stands of prickly pear, pincushion, and cholla cactus. Beyond were palo verdes, hackberries, and even a couple of cottonwood trees. A creek was nearby. Bright orange flowers were starting to bud on the long fingers of ocotillo and gnarled deep green branches of buckhorn cholla. Even the ubiquitous creosote looked greener. I could see why the land had appealed to Dana's old man. An ancient wooden gate parted a long, disheveled fence of barbed wire. Behind it, maybe half a mile away, was a smooth butte the shape of a fez. I parked the Crown Vic in front of the gate and was grateful to stretch my legs.

Dana said the property was an even thousand acres. As the desert floor swept up to the butte, it became craggier and strewn with burned-looking boulders the size of a Mini Cooper. Closer to me, it was especially thick with the yellow-white fuzz of teddy bear cholla. Jumping cactus. It made me glad I didn't go out in the desert like a tourist from the Midwest—in shorts. The land was utterly silent. It was almost a frightening sensory experience for a city boy. Although the soil was dry and the sky was bright blue with fluffy February clouds, the ground smelled of rain.

The gate was no problem. Although it still kept watch with a rusty chain and padlock, one post had pulled away enough for me to slip through. I walked along a trail toward the butte. Sure, I could have tried to bring out a team of forensic specialists. But that would have required permission from Peralta. And I was supposed to be writing his damned book. And I didn't know what I thought of the letter. An old man's ravings—stranger things had been imagined by the dying and committed to paper. I didn't know what the hell I was doing.

The trail took me through the cactus stands and across the undulating, sunblasted ground. In a few months, it could be fatal to be out here. Today, it was cool—almost chilly to thin-blooded Arizonans. I liked it, though. The old Boy Scout in me couldn't help but think of rattlesnakes and listen for a telltale sound. But the snakes were hibernating, and all I heard was the breeze through the arms of the ocotillo and my boots scuffing against the rocks and sand. The ground was dry. The rain of the previous night had spurned this place. I walked alone surrounded by nothing made by man.

My plan was to look around. Look around, go back and talk to Dana. And then turn her over to the sheriff's detectives. Maybe Peralta was right—I was doing any task to avoid sitting before that blank computer screen and writing. A task like seeking an old homicide victim in a thousand acres of wilderness. But the instructions in the letter were true. I walked a couple of hundred yards on the trail, heading for the butte. Then, as promised, I found a metal fence post, alone in the ground. Turning left, I could see an odd break in the ground, off to my right.

I wandered toward it, and in a moment an arroyo appeared. It was maybe 20 feet deep and held a dry wash. But its walls were steep and sudden. I didn't want to stand too close to the edge. The arroyo's edge was flush with the desert floor. A casual hiker would never know it was here. I started thinking of the hidden canyons where the Apache had eluded the cavalry. And then I saw a formation of bowling-ball-sized rocks exactly the shape and size of a man. They were maybe ten feet from the arroyo edge, and on the hard dirt of the desert floor. I looked around for similar sized stones, and none were nearby. These had been placed here. For a grave.

That was when I heard footsteps.

"This is private property."

The voice went with a giant. I'm six feet two, and I swear my eyes were on the level of his chest. With him, was a skinny kid wearing a football jersey bearing the lettering GHETTO.

I started to speak and the giant shoved me to the ground. My hand blazed in pain at breaking my fall against an outcropping of shale. But that was nothing compared to the kick in the ribs, and then I felt cholla biting into my arm. The kid was laughing, a high-pitched keening. I tried to roll off the cactus, but something sharp erupted into my stomach. I saw a large hiking boot flash between the ground and me.

Then I wasn't seeing anything.

# Chapter Six

By the time I made it home, the sky was rippling in deep scarlets and oranges. It would be a sunset for the record books, but right that moment I just wanted a martini with Lindsey. My right hand was on fire from the jumping cactus, and my left side felt as if it had been caved in by a rockslide. I kept touching it, and was surprised my ribs were still there. But every time I touched it, a bolt of pain zagged across my chest and up my neck. So much for helping old students. No good deed goes unpunished.

The lights were already on, glowing warmly through the picture window that faces Cypress Street. But when I came through the door, I heard muffled sobs. A look around the archway into the living room, and I saw Lindsey and Robin sitting close. Lindsey's arm was around her sister, who had her head down and was hunched forward on her elbows. I quietly closed and locked the front door, and took the right turn into the hallway that led to our bedroom, there, to pick out the remaining cactus spines with tweezers and take stock of my mess of an afternoon.

When I'd come to, I was about an inch from the edge of the arroyo. I was still woozy, and the wrong twist would have deposited me two stories down into the wash bed. I was surprised my attackers hadn't thought of it. But they were gone. As I spat a mouthful of bile into the sand and tried to rise, I could hear a distant buzz. Motorcycles, or all-terrain vehicles. Fading away.

By the time Lindsey came in, I had washed the worst of the desert off me. I managed to kiss her and let her snuggle into my arms without getting my ribs involved or letting her take hold of my injured hand. She offered to make martinis, and I let her.

"Do you feel better about Robin now?" I asked, after we had settled on the leather sofa that faced the picture window.

"Oh, Dave," she said, a small smile. She lithely swung her legs onto my lap while hanging onto her drink, and lolled her head back against the arm of the sofa.

"Are you all right?" She must have noticed I winced. I said I was. I was getting better at least. Despite a kick in the stomach, my system eagerly accepted the gin.

She said, "I guess I feel a little better. I know I've been acting weird. Seeing her for the first time in years…it brought back a lot. But time really can help things."

"You don't have to tell me."

"Dave, you know I have to tell you everything." She sipped her drink and ran one of her long, elegant fingers around the rim of her glass. "She's my half-sister, you know? She had a different dad. She's two years younger, but by the time she came along, Linda was already living with some new guy. I know you think it's weird to call my mother by her first name…"

"No," I said. "From the way you describe it, you kind of had to raise her."

"The dutiful daughter Lindsey," she said, an ambiguous shade in her voice. "Robin was a sweet girl, so creative. That all changed. She got into drugs by the time she was about thirteen. It didn't help that we moved to a new school every year, and Linda always had some new man she was self-destructing over. You've heard this a million times."

"I didn't know you had a sister," I said gently.

She sighed. "I know. I'm sorry." I stroked her feet with my free hand. In a moment, she continued. "For so many years, I felt like an orphan. When I found you, I just didn't want to dredge all that up. I never thought I'd see her again." She took an uncharacteristic gulp of her drink. "When I was twenty-five, I was leaving the Air Force. And Robin showed up. It was bad. She was still doing drugs, lying. Oh, Dave. My family sounds like a white trash reality show. I'm not like them. But I knew Robin was going to turn out just like Linda. God, I knew that when I was fifteen years old." By this time her eyes were full of tears.

"We don't choose our families, darling," I said. "I was lucky. But even so, I lost my parents when I was a baby. Then I lost my grandparents. Sometimes I almost wish some long lost brother or sister would arrive."

"I chose you," she said. "And I had a good visit with Robin. Maybe she has changed. Everybody gets older, and some people even grow up. She went back to college. My gosh, she's lived in New York and Paris. She sounds very accomplished."

"I'd call that a change for the better."

"Me, too," she said. "So when Robin showed up at the door today, I either had to treat her like the enemy, or like my sister." Lindsey says "eye-ther" and I say "eeth-er"; somehow we worked the whole thing out. She said, "So I invited her in, and we talked. I always wanted to save Robin. But I couldn't make her save herself. Now I think that's happened. Do you think I'm a fool?"

"Definitely not," I said. "You have a kind heart that I love."

"Oh, Dave…" And she was in my arms before I knew it. I let out something between a gasp and a yelp, and the remains of the martini flew onto the floor.

"Dave, what's wrong? Stop that—leave the martini glass alone. I'll get that later. What's wrong? Are you hurt?"

"No…yes…" And so I told her.

"Oh, my God…we're going to the ER…" This as she was taking an inventory of the dark red crescent spreading across my side and my swollen hand and arm. Then we fussed back and forth—I wasn't going to wait for eight hours in an overrun Phoenix emergency room. I promised I'd call the doctor in the morning if things got worse. Lindsey said I'd call the doctor no matter what.

"I feel like such a dolt," I said.

"They assaulted a deputy sheriff!"

"Oh, yeah, Mr. Tough Cop."

"Were you armed, Dave?"

I shook my head.

"Oh, God, they might have killed you. What if they had been armed?"

Then I tried to distract her by making a fresh martini for me, while telling her about the visit from Dana Underwood and her father's letter.

"Do you remember her?"

I shook my head. "Maybe I remember her voice. I don't know."

"She's a strawberry blonde, Dave," Lindsey teased. "You used to have a weakness for those strumpets."

"I have a weakness for you. And she looks like some soccer mom from Ahwatukee."

"Soccer moms can be hot," she said.

I said, "*Cherchez la femme.*" Lindsey wrinkled her nose. "Look for the woman. The subtle power of a woman."

Then, a teasing gleam came into her blue eyes: "Did you ever sleep with your students, professor?" By this time, we were at the built-in breakfast booth at the back of the kitchen.

"Do you really want to know?"

"I'm not sure." Lindsey was something of a moralist, in a gentle way.

"Well, I didn't sleep with my students. Although that certainly happens."

"Dr. Mapstone, the dutiful teacher. But, Dave, you really think there's a body out there?"

"I saw those rocks. And the father wrote in the letter that he buried this 'Z' under rocks. They could have sat undisturbed there for forty years, the place is so isolated."

"Except today."

"Except today," I agreed. "And what the hell were they doing out there, saying 'private property,' when that land belongs to Dana."

"Maybe they're really aggressive real-estate agents."

"Maybe," I said, and sipped the martini. "But nobody gets killed over real estate. Not even in Arizona."

"So what are you going to do now? Tell Peralta?"

"Are you kidding? He'll go postal. I don't need to be reminded again, in his special way, what a complete failure I am. I'm going to quietly turn it over to the detectives. I'm going to call her and have her come in and make a statement, then go back to my book work."

"Well, call her now. Maybe you can find out who those goons were. Then, I can nurse you with a healthy dinner. Later, I'll examine your privates, just to make sure they came through your ordeal. It might take some time…"

So after I finished my drink, I retrieved Dana's phone number from my old black briefcase, and sat in the study to call her. When Lindsey came in, she saw my face.

"What's wrong, History Shamus?"

"The number she gave me is wrong. It goes to Arturo's Llantera in Mesa."

"Maybe she's a big wheel."

"Ha-ha. I'm sure that's the number she gave me. Now I dial it and get a hubcap store. I tried the phone book—no Dana Underwood."

It made no damned sense, but I was already thinking what Lindsey now said.

"Maybe she didn't want you to contact her again."

# Chapter Seven

I leaned against the fender of the Crown Vic and watched a county jail inmate walk past with a shovel. Except for the orange jumpsuit, he looked nice enough. Those are the ones who will bash in your brains with the shovel and drive away with your county-issue vehicle. This guy only wanted to use the latrine. He set his shovel on the ground and climbed into the porta-john with all the gravity of an astronaut preparing to leave the moon. The porta-john had a sheriff's star on it, was painted in sheriff's office colors, and towed by a sheriff's cruiser. It went with the chain gang that was five hundred feet away removing the cairn-shaped boulders that might be the grave of a man known only as "Z."

Once again the lush desert spread out in every direction, with our view drawn to the misshapen butte, the result of a lava flow that was way outside my expertise to discuss. Sweeping up toward the butte, the ground seemed planed smooth, as if carved by some desert glacier that had left behind all manner of geological debris. I kicked the heel of my boot into the soil: too hard to bury anything without heavy equipment or more time and patience with hand implements than murder usually allows. The inmate retrieved his shovel and went back to where the desert floor suddenly collapsed into the hidden arroyo. Coming from that direction was Sheriff's Detective Patrick Blair.

"Dr. Mapstone," he said in his annoying sportscaster voice. "I should have known you'd be to blame for this adventure."

In his mid-thirties, Patrick Blair bore a vague resemblance to any number of dark-haired male movie stars of the moment: Jude Law, Ethan Hawke, Orlando Bloom, Matt Damon. They all ran together for me. He had definitely fallen into the deep end of the gene pool. For several years, he'd been a star of the homicide bureau. He'd worked with Lindsey on the Harquahala Strangler case, one of those cases you'd call notorious. This was when Lindsey and I were dating on and off, and then we were off for a few months. All while she was working with Patrick Blair. This left me with an irrational, childish, but unshakable dislike of the man. Seeing him, my ribs and back began to ache worse. When he got close enough, he held out the letter from Dana's father, now enclosed in an evidence bag.

"Where did you get this?"

"I told you on the phone, Blair. A woman came to my office, said she was a former student. After her father died, she found this letter. It contained a confession for a murder in 1966 and directions to the body."

"But you don't know who the victim is?"

"No."

"And you don't know the dead father's name?"

I shook my head. He was enjoying this too damned much.

"And now you can't find her."

"Right," I said, feeling more foolish. Maybe I should have said nothing, thrown Dana's letter in the trash, ignored the odd coincidence of getting my ass kicked in the location to which Dana—or whatever her name was—had led me. It didn't seem like the right thing to do. "What has your chain gang found?"

"They're just the brute labor, Mapstone," he said. "We've got detectives and evidence technicians standing by if we find anything. Which seems like a hell of a long shot. Lot of county resources being diverted out here…"

"I'm sure they'd call you if you needed to go back to the city for a facial or something."

He touched his cheek briefly. He said, "You're an asshole. You find a lot of trouble for an egghead. I was talking to the Phoenix detectives about the murder down in the 'hood, by your house. Ice pick into the brain. That'll do you." I fantasized about setting his youthful face on fire and putting it out with an ice pick. He went on. "These guys said the pick had been filed down so it was about three inches, and really sharpened. Just long enough to go through the ear into the brain, stir quickly and remove. That's cold blooded. Did you know the guy?"

I shook my head.

"He owned some check-cashing outlets," Blair said. "You ask me, they're bloodsuckers, taking the money of these poor Mexicans. And some of 'em are used by smugglers to launder money. So there's your case. He pissed somebody off, and they did him." Blair made a jab with his right hand into an imaginary head cradled in his left hand. So much for Peralta's straight eye for the gay crime.

"Sounds like something Bobby Hamid would do," Blair continued. "If we could ever make a charge stick against him."

"I thought he'd become a venture capitalist," I said. "That's what he says."

"Yeah, sure." Blair made an unhandsome snorting sound. I looked to see if snot had emerged from his perfect nose. "He's just as dirty as Sheriff Peralta has always said."

"More than you would know…" I said.

He looked at me sharply, then asked, "How's Lindsey?"

Before I could answer, or even feel a rush of male jealousy, there was a commotion off through the creosote bushes. A uniformed deputy emerged and gestured for us to come. I followed Blair, my hands instinctively pulling in, even though I was steering well clear of the numerous cholla and prickly pear. My arm was still red from cactus needles. We walked up the trail and turned at the lone, rusting metal fence post. Once again I could see the edge of the hidden drop. Now a deputy was starting to string yellow crime-scene tape, and another burly uniform with a shotgun was leading the inmates out. Seeming to follow them was a foul, telltale odor. A man who looked like Patrick Blair's twin brother met us.

"Hello, Mapstone," Detective Tony Snyder said, then, "Patrick, we got a body. Mapstone, you can leave. No way has he been there forty years."

I ignored him and followed them. Approaching the dead is just another cop task, even if you're the guy who works on forty-year-old homicides. And I'd seen some nasty scenes in the five years I spent as a patrol deputy, what now seems so many years ago. But I guess I never got used to it. My legs seemed heavier as we walked the final fifteen feet. About a third of the rocks had been removed. Most of the grave was still covered, but I guessed that Snyder had stopped the inmate labor for fear of contaminating what was now a crime scene. The excavated rocks sat lined up like deformed eggs. Beyond them, something had been uncovered. Blair was snapping on latex gloves and bending to look into a shallow pit.

I could see a head and the top of a torso, lying face up. The stones had done some damage, but enough was recognizable. It was a man with a small white moustache. Just lying there staring up at the flawless Arizona sky on a perfect winter day. Just like he was lying by the pool at the Sanctuary, waiting for a drink with an umbrella in it. Except his eyes were gone, replaced by things I didn't want to think about too much. And his ears were well chewed. The Sonoran Desert was full of critters small enough to skitter through rocks just as if they were weaving through rush-hour traffic on the way to dinner. And his skin was green, and the consistency of a dried tortilla, something the resorts definitely frown upon. And his view was spoiled by the boyish, handsome features of Patrick Blair and Tony Snyder studying him. It was all wrong.

# Chapter Eight

Napoleon said he wanted lucky generals. I couldn't tell if my luck was getting better or worse. A likely homicide victim had been discovered in Maricopa County—that was a plus. The sheriff was distracted elsewhere, so he wouldn't be bothered with more concern about my writing habits—definite plus. But then there was the missing Dana, no phone number, no address. That was my carelessness. Big minus. And the timetable. This was no historic crime; the body had been there for no more than a few weeks. I could just walk away. That was good, right? I had other things to do. It seemed smart not to push my luck. I walked back to the car and started out to the highway.

About a mile down the dusty road, the desert started to roll and the vegetation became nothing but spindly creosote bush. I was thinking about Dana. This pleasant nobody woman. I could run her name through the Miami University alumni association. Maybe I also should check the NCIC—maybe she had a record beyond a college transcript. But I had a gut feeling, the part of my gut that wasn't still aching from the impact of a large boot, that I wasn't going to find her. So the question was why she put on the pose. We'd find easily enough who really owned the land. No, I corrected myself. Blair and Snyder would find it. I was free.

That's when I saw something bobbing above the brush. Something moving. I slowed the car so I wasn't making a dust trail, and rolled down the window. That buzz again of ATVs. My body kicked up the panic juice. It's amazing how one beating can make you feel more afraid. Make you feel vulnerable and old. Funny old Mapstone, it was probably just some kids out for a harmless ride. I was about to roll the window back up and get going when there was a break in the creosote brush, and I saw them. They were about five hundred yards away, and moving on an angle toward the road. Somehow I thought I would pick out the giant if he had been five miles away. I looked at the police radio hanging from the dashboard. Reached for the microphone, heard it scrape out of its metal clip. Then I put it back. My mouth was suddenly dry. It had been years since I'd had a drop of water. I made myself slow my breathing and make a plan.

This time I made sure to make dust. I drove about half a mile, keeping an eye on the pair, then stopped in the middle of the road. There wasn't much time. I stepped out of the car and grabbed the three-cell black Maglite from the passenger seat. By then, the two ATVs muscled into the road, leaving behind four tracks indelible in the ancient desert soil. They stopped on the other side of the car and slowly dismounted. Gunfighters dropping from their horses—although a quick scan showed no shooting irons. This time I had a better look at them. Not being face down in the dirt getting kicked will allow that. The younger one still had on a white football jersey with GHETTO in blue letters. Obviously no time for laundry out here. He looked about twenty, had a sandy buzz cut and a mouth that looked prone to drooling, and probably thought the girls adored him. The big one didn't look so big on second viewing. He wouldn't stand out in a big-city skyline. He had that pumped up look you get courtesy of the state prison system. Besides the black mullet, the other thing I noticed was his eyes. Worlds could be lost in those eyes.

They started around the car from different directions. I walked to the rear, toward the giant. I had no time for David and Goliath musings, although as I recalled, David had superior technology. By the time we met at the back bumper, I had my right side away from him, just the way I wanted it. He started, "You don't…" But by that time I had made an uppercut into his crotch and the Maglite was attached to my hand. He let out a massive burst of breath, foul enough for me to smell it. Next I jammed the heavy steel flashlight into his ribs, a pain center they teach you at the academy, if not in academia. And he was on the way down to the blond desert dirt.

I wheeled on the kid and had the Colt Python .357 Magnum in my hands.

"Get on the fucking ground!" I commanded, trying to lower and steady my voice. My blood was up and I was barely containing my own terror. So I was careful to keep my finger outside the trigger guard, unless he gave me a reason to shoot him. He was about one second from giving me a reason, but he immediately stopped, and pissed his pants. I could actually hear it, then see a large dark stain spread down the leg of his khaki cargo pants. He stuttered something. I backed away so I could keep an eye on both of them.

"Reach in that car and get the handcuffs that are in the glove box. If you take more than five seconds, I'll shoot you."

"Yessssir…" Ghetto stammered, and did as I asked him.

"Now, get down on the ground, facing me, face down. Do it now."

When he was face down in the road, I moved closer to the heap that had been Goliath. He was on his knees, in a kind of face-down fetal-position, moaning. I kicked him in the side as hard as I could.

"Were you going to say I don't listen too good? My boss says that all the time." I would face the police brutality charge later. I needed him to stay down. And my foot felt broken from the impact with his tree-trunk of a body. I walked over and retrieved the handcuffs from Ghetto.

"If you stand up I'll shoot you. If you roll over I'll shoot you. If you look up I'll shoot you."

"Yesssssir."

"Keep your goddamned face down in the dirt. Shut up."

I holstered the Python and cuffed the giant, barely. I double-locked the handcuffs. As a young deputy, I had seen big guys break out of handcuffs. But he didn't seem to be going anywhere. Then I popped the trunk, found another set of cuffs and did the kid.

"Stand up, get your feet under you." I leaned him against the car, facing me. After I read him his rights, he was wide-eyed.

"You're a cop? We didn't know."

"Well now you know."

"We'd a never…"

"Oh, you just beat up civilians?"

"It's private property…" He was starting to blubber. My heart was hard.

"What are you doing out here?"

"We're supposed to keep people away, that's all…"

"It's a hell of a way to do it." I searched for enough saliva to speak. My mouth was a dry wash bed.

"I didn't want to hurt you. It was Nelson." He nodded toward the giant.

"Why are you supposed to keep people away?"

He gave a great sniffle and said, "I can't tell you, dude. I can't…"

I watched him for a minute, then said. "Everything you've heard about prison rape is true." I watched his eyes. "Good-looking kid like you. They're going to have a field day. Assaulting a police officer—you're going to be in prison until you're an old man…"

I opened the car door and started to push him into the back seat.

"No," the kid sobbed. His head was so far down on his chest it looked like it might just roll off into the road. I leaned him against the car, also keeping an eye on Nelson.

"If I help you, can I get off easier?"

Amazing the influence of television; everybody knew their roles when the police came calling. Unless the kid had done this before. "Maybe. Depends on your record."

"I'm clean. I swear to God." He sniffled and gulped, a sickening sound. Then he said, "We were hired by Jack Fife."

"Who is that?"

"He's some kind of private security dude who works for a land company. Has this big office in North Scottsdale. He told us to keep this land clear. Said it was private property."

"Why was he so worried? It's miles from anything."

"I don't know, dude. I swear to God."

By that time a sheriff's cruiser was pulling in behind me. I had something I wanted hauled downtown. Later I would have time to be afraid, to sit alone and feel the point of panic in my middle, to wonder why the hell I hadn't just sat and called for backup. But even then, I would feel good about my luck.

# Chapter Nine

The city kept growing. Forty-eight thousand new houses a year. One hundred twenty thousand new residents annually. Five hundred square miles of urban area with Phoenix, the nation's fifth largest city, surrounded by two dozen suburbs and two Indian reservations. They called the suburbs "boomburbs": Gilbert from 10,000 to 200,000 in twenty years; Mesa, with 450,000 people, now larger than the cities of St. Louis, Minneapolis, or Atlanta. To accommodate all this, the growth machine that is the Phoenix economy ate at least two acres of desert every hour. The swimming pools and golf courses, landscaping and water taps consumed millions of gallons of water daily, virtually all coming from manmade reservoirs and canals. The experts predicted only more growth. But all that seemed somehow removed from my life. I was embedded in the old city—old meaning the part of town that existed prior to 1950. I lived in a 1924 house and worked in a courthouse that was built in 1929, right on the brink of the Great Depression.

The gentle months slipped away. So did the immediate memory of my adventure in the Harquahala Desert. My assailants were quickly fed into the criminal justice thresher, with only a few dozen hours of my time spent writing reports and testifying. The big guy was going home—he'd spent half his life in prison for assault and robbery. The kid was another sad loser who never got past eighth grade and washed out of construction jobs. The detectives told me they were cheap help hired by a land company that owned adjacent property to keep out illegal dumping—and of course the company considered them independent contractors and was fully indemnified against such uh-ohs as assaulting a deputy sheriff. The fools hadn't even been protecting the right property.

The body turned into another bizarre Arizona story. He was Harry Bell, the landowner, aged eighty-two. Not a "Z" to be found—Harry's middle name was Truman and he drove rock and gravel trucks for a living. He convinced his brother to bury him out there when he died, as he did in his sleep in a trailer in a dusty lot in a little hamlet named Hyder, southwest of the city. It was Harry's last wish, to rest on the land he owned. Stranger things have happened in my state. The writer Edward Abbey, who hated modern man's incursions into the desert, is said to be buried somewhere on the north rim of the Grand Canyon, in a hidden grave dug by his friends. Bell's autopsy turned up nothing unusual, the detectives seemed satisfied, and if the county attorney prosecuted anyone I never heard about it.

Harry Bell had no children, only an ex-wife he hadn't seen in thirty years and a brother. No daughter named Dana. There was no record of a Dana Underwood in the Miami University alumni association, and the Dana Watkins the association showed was twenty-four years old and living in New England—too young to be my soccer mom on the edge of middle age. Why she came to me and sent me on an errand to find the body of Harry Bell—I had no answers. With Peralta demanding to see a manuscript, I decided not to press the matter. The mysterious Dana became a statement in a detective's file, although Patrick Blair didn't keep her "father's" letter. So I dropped it in a rarely opened desk drawer. It was my "get to it someday" file. It was a full drawer.

The gentle months slipped away. I received no more broadsides from the county supervisors. Lindsey and I were looking forward to our first real vacation in years: a late-June train trip across the Canadian Rockies. It was an indulgence we shouldn't have considered, so of course we did. Until then, we reveled in our nights and weekends on Cypress Street. Lindsey had her gardens, where she exploited the long growing season and out-witted the merciless sun. When she came in sweaty and covered in dirt, she was gorgeous. The evening often meant martinis on the patio, where we talked about our day and solved the world's problems. At night, we read to each other, often in bed, where she would drape a leg across me. We went through Graham Greene's *Travels with My Aunt* and David Kennedy's *Freedom from Fear*. The tamale women came to the door every Monday night and we bought a dozen each time. I gave Lindsey backrubs every night before bed. We walked to Encanto Park, and went to spring training games, which Lindsey loved.

Nearly all marriages, even happy ones, are mistakes. Somebody said that—Tolkien, I think. I didn't take anything for granted. But I liked to think we had both met at a point in our lives where we didn't have anything to prove, where we knew that what was rare and precious couldn't be valued in money. I knew I not only loved Lindsey, but I liked her and admired her.

My days fell into a comforting routine. If I was working at the office, I took the bus down Central to Washington, then walked to the courthouse. At home, I sat at Grandfather's old desk, in the study that opened off the western end of the living room. I picked a dozen of the cases I had been handed since coming back home to Phoenix and being given a job by Peralta. Back then these had just been cases gathering dust in the records bureau, ignored by the cold-case detectives.

At first, he had taken pity on me. I knew that. I was recently divorced and denied tenure. I never intended to stay. But I found that I had a knack for the work. At least that's what I hoped, outside the moments, which were many, when I felt like a fraud in two worlds, academia and law enforcement. Having a county supervisor take a bead on me only reinforced that insecurity. Still, I recalled cases such as the murder in the 1950s of the mining executive. It hadn't been solved by DNA, or the autopsy, or cop luck. It was solved when, four decades later, I had applied a historian's touch. That key statement—it was untrustworthy because the supposed witness was a business rival, even an enemy, and was not even in the city on that date. Then I had found the investigating officer's notes—primary sources—which contradicted the press reports—secondary sources. Those discoveries had turned me toward a new interpretation of the sad events, then evidence—enough to indict, if the suspect had not gone on to a tougher court years before. Sure, a skeptical detective or journalist might have done the same. But I had done it two dozen times now with success. Recalling it made me feel better about these four years back at the Sheriff's Office, and more secure against the attacks of county supervisors.

For the book, I went through those case files again, crimes from 1932 and 1948 and 1959. Wearing headphones and listening to jazz CDs, I organized research and outlined chapters. Lindsey had set me up with a new Macintosh laptop, but I still loved working through paper files, making notes on cards and legal pads. Then, music off, I started writing. It was like grad school again, without the student loans. Once I settled down to the work, I found myself enjoying the writing. At night, during cocktails, I would read the manuscript to Lindsey. Sometimes I imagined returning to history writing—and not the tedious, statistic-laden stuff I had been forced to write to get published as an academic. David Hackett Fischer's *Washington's Crossing* was on my desk at work, and in spare moments I went through it—pure pleasure!—and wondered if I could do as well.

It was the second Thursday in May when Peralta sat in my office as I read a few chapters. One of the big windows was open because the sheriff had brought two Cuban cigars, Cohibas. It was against at least a page of county rules, but I wasn't complaining. It gave him something to do instead of stopping me to question a minor word choice or make a suggestion I hated. Finally, he sat contentedly wreathed in tobacco smoke, closed his eyes and listened. The old office seemed at home with men smoking cigars.

"Maybe it's time for me to retire, Mapstone."

I stopped reading and looked at him. Then I laughed. He just stared at me with his coal-black eyes until I stopped.

"You ever hear of Mara 18?"

"A gang," I said.

"Yeah, well…" He let some ash fall off his cigar and let it sit in the ashtray, a little Cuban smokestack industry on my desk. "I'd call it a terrorist organization. Mara 18 started in LA. Back in the '70s it was Mexican immigrants. Then in the '80s, they started recruiting Centro Americanos—all these rootless young men who came here to get away from the wars down there. Only this wasn't the Boys and Girls Club. Their big enemy is the Salvatruchas—that's mostly Central American, Salvadoran, you know."

"They're operating over here?" I asked.

"Don't let the chamber of commerce know," he said. He took his cigar again, took a puff, kept it in his hand. "A little before seven this morning, a carload of Mara 18 gets out at an apartment, it's in a county island over by Tolleson. They go in and kill five people. Only four of those people are under six years old."

"God…" It was all I could say.

"None of the neighbors wanted to talk, of course. Nobody wants to talk and get killed. But there's a utility crew working across the street. They said the guys in the car had tattoos on their faces, their foreheads. That's the way these gang members look." He rubbed his eyes, then slowly shook his head. "Turns out, the apartment was being used by Salvatruchas—but of course the men aren't there. How long before we get a retaliatory hit on Mara 18? A day? A week? Places in this town are like Baghdad, or the West Bank." He sighed and watched the tip of the cigar.

"I get tired of this shit, Mapstone," he said, in a tone of voice I had never heard from him before, a far-away voice. "It's like the world is just crazy. And what kind of future do I have anyway?"

"Governor Peralta has a nice ring to it," I said.

"Not in this state," he said. "Maybe I need a change. I could be making money in real estate, just like everybody else."

"As you said to me about teaching, 'you'd be bored,'" I said. "You were born to be the sheriff of Maricopa County."

He was about to say something when the door opened. Lindsey and Robin came in laughing.

# Chapter Ten

That night I dreamed of men with tattoos on their faces. Blue ink was etched into their foreheads and cheeks. I couldn't read the words, but they were in English, not Spanish. The tattooed men were digging a grave in the desert, then they were trying to bury me in the grave, slamming bowling-ball-sized rocks onto me, and the rocks didn't hurt but I was fighting for my life in dream slo-mo. I couldn't breathe. Then I was in our bedroom, watching the bluish moonlight coming in from the street. The only sound was Lindsey's quiet, regular breathing. I put my hand on her hip, and let her warm, soft skin reassure me that this was reality.

It had not been a nightmare-inducing day. In fact, it had been a good day. Peralta had made only minor suggestions on the chapters. The cigar was fine, although I could still taste its bitter aftermath, even after two teeth-brushings and one swig of mouthwash. No reason to feel anxiety, aside from a potential lecture from the dentist. As I lay there, my heart still pounding from the dream, I wondered if I had somehow let Peralta down. His talk of retiring, of being worn out by the increasing madness of politics and society, was so unlike him that I thought he was joking. But he doesn't joke. Maybe I should have tried to get him to talk more. Maybe I should have invited him over for a cocktail. No, that wouldn't do. He was probably on some riff that had nothing to do with his doubts or fears or interior life. Mike Peralta had none of those things. It was what had finally busted up his marriage. It wasn't up to me to try to reach him, not after nearly a quarter century of friendship. The cornerstone of that friendship was my willingness to let him be.

We were interrupted anyway. Lindsey and Robin were on their way to the Biltmore to shop. Robin had become more of a fixture of those spring months, as Lindsey had little by little set her caution aside. I had learned that Robin's last name was Bryson, that she rode a motorcycle, and had a master's degree from the University of Delaware, where she had specialized in the WPA Art Project. This had brought her to the attention of a very wealthy retired cookie magnate in Paradise Valley, who collected paintings, murals, and posters from the Social Realism movement, among other enthusiasms. From power to the workers to collectibles for the capitalists. Robin lived with her boyfriend, Edward, in a bungalow down in the Roosevelt District. We had not yet met this Edward, who was an artist. As Lindsey had spent more time with Robin, it had seemed like a good thing. Lindsey had never been one to pal around with the girls, just as I had few male friends after college. A woman friend, a lost sister who had gotten her act together, was something new, and Lindsey seemed to like it.

In my office, introductions were made and Peralta was unusually charming. As they talked, I studied the two women, searching for the sisterly similarities. They were both about the same height. This day, Lindsey was dressed in a white sleeveless knit top and black cotton skirt coming to just above her knees. Robin was wearing blue jeans and a vivid tie-dyed work shirt. Her newsboy cap from our first encounter was gone and her hair was loose. It was a thicker and wilder than Lindsey's hair, fell below her shoulders, and was somewhere between light brown and blond. Robin was tan, while Lindsey was fair. She had gray eyes to Lindsey's blue. Her features were more closely clustered, and her eyes deeper-set. Somehow her features didn't assemble quite right, although they could be attractive when she was speaking, when her face became mobile and expressive. Yet they had the same mouth, dimples, chin. When they sat side by side, talked and laughed and glanced—there was connective tissue, in their eyes, and in glances and identical smiles.

"What does a private curator do?" Peralta was sitting on the edge of the desk, and I swear he was sucking in his gut. It was a most un-Peralta like curiosity, and Lindsey gave me a secret smile.

"She arranges the sex toys of the filthy rich," Robin said, nodding her head in slow seriousness.

"I always suspected," Peralta said, and the room boomed with his unaccustomed laughter. Robin tended to be as off-the-wall boisterous as Lindsey was subtle and ironic.

"I help guide the collector," Robin said. "In art, that is."

"The rich guy," Peralta said.

"Right. His collection is focused on Social Realism and he's interested in WPA-era stuff, but he also has some awesome Latin American paintings. Part of my job is to research the art scene. I'm in contact with the galleries, sometimes with artists themselves. I run a lot of interference. Some of the galleries can be really obnoxious."

"Kind of like Mapstone, here," Peralta said.

"David is interesting." Robin smiled at me. "I've never had a brother-in-law before."

"So what else do you do?" Peralta asked.

"Some art can also be fraudulent, and I help him research a work he's looking to buy, making sure it's the real thing," Robin said. "I also keep his library of books and periodicals, and records on the collection, things like insurance appraisals and bibliographical information. Don't you yawn, now—this is not boring stuff! Sometimes I arrange for his work to be loaned to museums. Here's where it can get sweet. Last year, I got a great trip to Madrid for just one painting. Then some weeks I feel like I'm a moving company—he's got a house in Aspen and a penthouse in New York, besides the place in Paradise Valley. He's got a very cool jet…"

Peralta had as close to a rapt expression as his big immobile face could hold. It was fascinating. If I had launched into an exposition about the root causes of the Great Depression or the complex social changes of Renaissance Italy, Peralta would have been twitching after the second sentence. But I was not blond and long-legged, and Robin had a quirky charisma. She told a good story, had a big, uninhibited laugh, and looked at everyone she talked to with intense, friendly interest. When she was talking and laughing, the animation brought her face together in a way that was attractive. My biggest surprise was Peralta's interest.

"Who is this rich guy?" he asked. When she supplied the name, he nodded and exhaled. "Wish I could get him to contribute to my campaign."

"May I?" Robin snatched the cigar out of Peralta's hand, struck a dashing pose and took a puff. She said, "Cuban?"

He nodded approvingly, making no effort to retrieve it. I made an extravagant face at Lindsey, who raised her eyebrows and smiled. Freud said, sometimes a cigar is just a cigar. They went on talking and sharing the Cohiba.

There was a melancholy aspect to all this. For what seemed like my entire adult life, Peralta had been married to the same woman. In their heyday, Mike was rising to the top of the sheriff's office and Sharon was becoming the most popular radio shrink on the West Coast. I cared about both of them. Even when I was living away, I had always found a friendly place with them when I came back to Phoenix to visit. But they were never very similar and the gulf only widened over the years. Now Sharon was living in San Francisco, and the sheriff seemed happy to work all the time, just as he had through their marriage and the raising of two daughters. I missed Sharon, but she was doing well. And Peralta showing some interest in Robin was better than him sitting alone every non-working moment in the big house in Dreamy Draw.

I could almost hear their voices in the bedroom, as I lay in bed and my mind discarded the contents of the previous day. But then I was not fully awake. My mind was distracted by the bad dream. Gradually, I got that feeling in the belly that comes when you've been lying in bed, enjoying yourself, not quite with it, and then you remember the car has a flat tire or somebody said something you wished you hadn't heard. Robin's words came back to me. Robin did say it. I wasn't dreaming.

The conversation was on how the sisters had reunited. Robin and Lindsey took turns telling about that day in the neighborhood, when we had been called to the crime scene. This brought an update from Peralta on the homicide, him being a grand master of information, whether it's cop gossip or an interesting investigation going on in another department. The victim was a lawyer, but he also owned two dozen check-cashing outlets, the banks of choice of immigrant workers, as well as human smugglers—the coyotes—and sometimes drug traffickers. But his stores seemed pretty clean, Peralta said. They had passed muster with a state attorney general's investigation the previous year. Maybe somebody was trying to move in on him, get him to do illegal business or sell out. The victim had been forty-two years old, had lived in Willo for two years, and was named Alan Cordesman. And that's when Robin spoke.

"I knew him," she said.

# Chapter Eleven

"There's no history here, it's so new." People who moved to Phoenix from the Midwest often said that. That's what Dana, or whatever her name was, said. It's a lie, born of an inability to look beyond the brand-new houses they bought and the brand-new Wal-Mart down the road. Arizona has a richer and longer history than the places many of them considered home. Ancient Indian peoples created diverse cultures. Conquistadors and padres cut a trail for European settlement. Cowboys and Buffalo Soldiers, Confederates and Federals, Mormons and Chinese railroad builders, miners and Navajo code talkers. Nope, there's no history here. We also had our share of crime history. Dillinger came to Tucson thinking he could hide out from the small-town cops. He was wrong. Winnie Ruth Judd—the trunk murderess; now we know she was probably railroaded by the Phoenix elite, trying to cover up for one of their own. From the rustlers and bushwhackers of the nineteenth century to the international gangs of the twenty-first century, Arizona had always drawn badlands people.

One or more of them stuck an ice pick in my neighbor's brain. Only the police didn't have a suspect, and my sister-in-law Robin had known the victim.

"I knew him casually," she had said. "I met him on a First Friday, at a gallery down on Roosevelt. He seemed like a nice man…" Then she told a story about riding her motorcycle to Denver and stopping in every honky-tonk along the way to dance with a cowboy.

Later, Lindsey and I had talked about it. It was a conversation that didn't end well. Lindsey and I have few fights, and we're quick to seek mutual forgiveness. But I'd be damned if I knew how we got into this one. Toward the end, she seemed agitated but said I seemed agitated. And I felt misunderstood—that's just what she said I was doing to her position. Which was: Robin said she knew the guy, what's the big deal? "I didn't say it was a big deal," I said. "I just wonder if she should tell the police she knew him." She said, "She met him at a gallery with a hundred other people. Dave, you're being paranoid." We went on this way for fifteen minutes, when Lindsey said something I had never heard her say before, "I just can't talk about this any more." And, uncharacteristically flushed and red-eyed, she got up and left the room.

Later, she hugged me close as I prepared to leave for work, and gave me enough of a French kiss to please a Parisian. But the encounter left me feeling a little raw. I remembered saying something about whether we should trust a woman who had a history of substance abuse. "That's not fair!" Lindsey came as close to a shout as I had ever heard her use in conversation. In a calmer voice, she said, "Robin is thirty-five years old, and she has ten clean years behind her." My blood was up by then, too, and it was an effort not to say, "she claims she has ten clean years." But I said nothing. I knew we would talk about it later.

The fight was still on my mind that afternoon as I left the Hayden Library at the university. I had spent the day surrounded by Hollinger boxes and files that contained source material for the book. Now, I walked down Cady Mall, past buildings that hadn't changed much since I was a student. The money went to biotech, business, and athletics, not liberal arts. It was hot enough to be uncomfortable, the sun reflecting intense light back from the sidewalk. But a breeze was blowing from the north, and coeds walked past in the latest incarnation of provocative miniskirts. I was the model of worldly discretion, marital fidelity yet appreciation.

Then I saw a slender, well-dressed man walking directly toward me. He saw me, so it was too late to switch course. I should have done so anyway. He was not the kind to wave. He merely held out his hands appreciatively and smiled.

"Dr. Mapstone, are you teaching again?"

"Hello, Bobby."

"You look so at home on campus, Dr. Mapstone," he said, and changed direction to fall in at my side.

"We shouldn't be seen talking," I said.

"And why should I not talk to you?" He had a slight English accent. "Because Sheriff Peralta has convinced you that I am the godfather of organized crime in Phoenix?"

I stopped and faced him. Bobby Hamid was wearing a navy pinstriped suit that covered his trim form with perfection. His lovely muted blue tie went with a white shirt that was dazzling in the sun. Not a molecule of sweat dared visit his movie-idol face. I faced him and said, "Look me in the eye and tell me it's not true."

He smiled, kept eye contact, and affirmed that it was not true. "But of course you do not believe me," he said. "You see it as a cheap trick of revisionist history. You have a strong loyalty to your friend, the sheriff. And in his anti-Persian bigotry, he cannot handle it that I, who came to this very campus as a foreign student, could become such a success. To me, an American success story involving a Middle Eastern man is nothing but good for our society today…"

"Yeah, yeah," I said, resuming my walk. Unfortunately, he matched my stride. "You're a venture capitalist, and an Episcopalian, and on the board of a dozen worthy charities."

"All true," he said. "Now I am not saying our city is without crime and corruption. Far from it. Things happen in Phoenix, Dr. Mapstone, and they seem inexplicable. But then you realize there's a certain, let us say, alignment of interests. The moneyed and political classes get their way. Funny thing. But those are the friends of your sheriff. I am happy to be an outsider from such things."

A flock of coeds walked by and Bobby asked, "So how is your book coming?"

By now I was sweating from frustration. "How do you know these things?" I said. Peralta had been convinced for years that Bobby had a mole inside the sheriff's office.

"I'm a big fan, Dr. Mapstone. Are you writing about my case?"

"Not until Peralta puts you away for many years," I grinned.

"Oh, David, please. You do the tough cop act so badly... although you seemed to protect yourself well enough when those two hoodlums assaulted you a few months back."

"Peralta is right. You've paid off a spy in the department."

"Not at all," he said. "I just hear things, keep up with the people I care about."

"How can I get off that list? Or, maybe given your reputation, forget that last request."

"I was talking about the Hayden Yarnell case," he went on. "It was one of your most remarkable. The grandsons of the famous rancher, kidnapped in the Great Depression and disappeared. Dr. Mapstone's greatest triumph, I would say."

"I remember it."

"And whatever happened to that lovely young woman you were seeing then, while you and Miss Lindsey were on the 'outs'?"

"I don't know," I said, too hurriedly.

"She seemed very sensual, very sure of herself—so American," he said. "Gretchen, I think her name was."

I just kept walking.

"Ah, well, I can understand you choosing Miss Lindsey, once she had tired of, what should we call it, 'testing the waters' with that handsome young detective. And you conceive yourself too American, too upright, to have taken Miss Gretchen as your mistress. I must confess, I might have had a hard time choosing between the two..."

"Bobby, what is your fucking point?"

"I'm sorry I upset you," he said, lightly touching my sleeve. "I just hoped that you were writing about the Yarnell case."

"Rest your worried mind," I snarled.

We walked in silence for a moment, then he said, "I am not one to seek anything to which I am not entitled. But I did save your life, David."

"You did."

"So the one time I really did shoot someone in the sheriff's jurisdiction was to save his best friend." He made a clicking sound with his tongue and teeth. By that time, we had reached the bus stop.

"Used any ice picks lately?" I asked.

"Such an imagination," he laughed. "Where are you parked?"

"I took the bus, Bobby."

"Very responsible." He applauded softly. "Soon we'll have light rail, and almost be like a real city. Well, I must be off." He insisted on shaking hands again. "I don't want to make the class wait. I'm teaching this semester, in the executive MBA program."

"Goodbye, Bobby."

He walked back into the campus. Then he turned, as if he had forgotten something. He said, "Do be careful out in the desert, Dr. Mapstone. And I can't wait to read my chapter in your book."

# Chapter Twelve

Counter-factual history. It's a fancy way of imagining things—say, if America had stayed isolationist during World War II and the Nazis had won, what kind of world would we be living in? Counter-factual history: What if Bobby Hamid had not appeared three years ago when a bad guy was about to put a bullet in my brain? My world would have been over. Bobby was a killer, and I owed him my life. What if I had stayed with Gretchen? No contest there—although why did I feel the flush of guilt over remembering her? It was a guilt that probably informed my intense dislike of Patrick Blair. Lindsey and I weren't together then. She had run away from me, remember? After we were back together, we hadn't compared notes about our time apart. We weren't the kind of couple who shared every detail, right down to the anatomical specifics, of our past lovers.

A future with Gretchen would have been impossible—she lived too many lies, carried too much darkness beneath them. It had been a crazy time in my life, and not surprisingly, the liaison with Gretchen had carried all the thrill of the temporary and the dangerous. What if Lindsey hadn't come back, come to my door that Christmas Eve? It was a history too bleak to contemplate. That winter of Gretchen and Lindsey—that was a story to tell another day.

The bus was passing the tattered oleanders of State Hospital, where the Trunk Murderess escaped twice, when my cell phone rang. The readout glared PERALTA.

"Where are you?" he demanded, with no preliminaries.

"On a bus."

There was a long pause.

"What are you doing on a bus, Mapstone?"

"Riding it."

"Are you crazy? What's your twenty?"

He was talking cop-speak. I told him my location.

"Get off now. I'll pick you up at 24th and Van Buren. If they don't throw you in the loony bin."

I hit the call button just in time, and was soon standing on the curb with the diesel fumes and the shopping-cart mumbler. I was still thinking of counter-factual history: What if I hadn't come back to Phoenix four years before? My world wouldn't exist at the whim of Mike Peralta.

In only ten minutes a shining black Ford Expedition pulled up. Peralta was using his driver today. I got in the back with him. He filled up his side of the seat, but his attention was focused on a file in his lap.

"Who is Louis Bell?" he asked, still reading.

I was in a brain fugue for a moment, then remembered sharply.

"He's the brother of a guy who was found dead in the desert," I said evenly.

"Harry Bell?"

"Right."

"You're a very bad boy, Mapstone. Finding dead bodies when you are supposed to be working on our book."

"Sorry," I said, staring at the red ears of the young deputy driving. I made myself take a quiet deep breath. There was no telling how the sheriff might react to the stimulus of insubordination, incompetence, or trying to sneak something past him. Put a gun in his face or a dying child at his feet and he's the calmest man on the planet. He has other moods, too.

"So tell me what led you to this body of Harry Bell?"

I went through it with him as we drove. I imagined the brother had somehow complained to the Sheriff's Office. Maybe he was mad that the chain gang tracked up the property, or a deputy had been rude. Maybe he was claiming we had robbed the corpse—I've seen civilians make worse charges. Sometimes they're true. So I told Peralta about the appearance of Dana What's-her-name, reminded him in fact that he had briefly seen her the day he was leaving my office. He refused to remember. I told him about Mrs. Every Soccer Mom, with her hands in her lap and her memories of me as a teacher. About the letter from her father, with a confession to homicide and precise directions to the body.

"Where are we going?" We were now on the Red Mountain Freeway, speeding past Tempe Town Lake.

Peralta set aside his folder and looked at me. His eyes were unreadable. "You'll see. You aren't the only one who gets to keep secrets."

"This wasn't a secret," I said. "I just didn't think…" I let the sentence trail off.

"Go on," he said. "You got the letter from the old man, and you went out to the desert. You find the body of this Harry Bell. Did you know him? Know his brother?"

"No and no."

"Go on." He opened a new file and started making notes with a gold pen.

I went on. But I was also wondering. Peralta had been a genuine friend to me over many years. Some days, though, I tired of his games, his pride in having people beholden to some transaction or obligation. I'm sure he wasn't even aware of them, as most of us are not fully self-aware. It was worse for him. Although he was brave and charming, he was also stubborn and, on so many fronts, shut down. His curiosity didn't extend beyond cop stuff and golf—even a younger interest in custom cars had been set aside. He didn't read books and was proud of it. He didn't know much beyond an encyclopedic knowledge of law enforcement, and wore that comfortably. In this, he was different from his late father, Judge Peralta, and from Sharon. They had been divorced for a year now. Without her, his worst tendencies seemed to come

out. I used to think Peralta was a throwback. But now I realized that he is the American male of the new century. I admired
Peralta for many things. But I wondered if I liked him.

By this time we were pulling off the Pima Freeway and enter-
ing a parking lot. It was smaller than a New England state, and
full of cars. Beyond was a dun-colored building that could have
been a Wal-Mart or a Best Buy. It was a big box—a big box of
gambling. Going a few hundred yards east of the Scottsdale city
limits made the difference. Casino Arizona was the economic
prize of the Salt River Indian Reservation. We were in a sovereign
nation, and also a part of suburban Phoenix. The city ended
abruptly and changed to fields—the Pima and Maricopa Indians
had been farming in Arizona for centuries. It was a good bet
they were related to the Hohokam, the ancient people who dug
the canals and settled in the valley that became Phoenix, and
then disappeared. No history here, remember? Fast forward to the
twenty-first century, where the sweet spot for these Indian nations
is the gambling addiction of the white-eyes. Indian gaming had
come to Arizona while I was living in California, and although I
was vaguely aware of casinos encircling Phoenix I had never been
in one. I was no prude. Gambling was one of the few vices I had
passed on when going through the devil's cafeteria line.

It was three p.m., but the parking lot was full. By the time we
pulled under the portico marked for valet parking, it was clear
Peralta was not thinking of an afternoon of blackjack. Several
tribal police cruisers sat bumper-to-bumper, flanked by sheriff's
vehicles and unmarked sedans. I turned to Peralta. The SUV
had stopped but he was getting out the door. I followed him
inside, past a cordon of tribal cops.

We walked through the lobby into a vast, dimly lit space.
It seemed that way, at least, after the intense sunlight outside.
Light came from row upon row of slot machines packed closely
together and from a discreet purple glow around the ceiling.
More light identified the Pima Lounge and Starz Bar. Then the
room opened into a large space under a circular ceiling. The
noise was overpowering, electronic pings, blips, and gurgles,

snatches of up-tempo songs that changed every few feet, nothing coherent, just a wave of unending sounds. All the sensory inputs were meant to focus on the business at hand. I recalled Grandfather's admonition that casinos were not built by the money of the winners.

We walked quickly past the machines, which looked high tech and elaborate—not at all my memory of slots. They had names like Xanadu, S'mores, Triple-Double Diamond, and Wild Thing, and comfortable seats were attached. Few were unattended. The crowd was mostly older and badly dressed, although that description embraced much of the population of Greater Phoenix. From the slack look of their faces, they could have been working in a textile mill. Nobody looked to be having a good time. None turned to notice as we walked through, escorted by two linebacker-sized tribal cops in uniform.

Then we were alone, stepping around a row of chairs that had been set up to block off a far province of the slots empire. More tribal police stood watch. Beyond them, all I could see was a circle of men wearing plainclothes and badges on their belts. One of them broke free: Patrick Blair. He looked at me with the suppressed glee of a tattling child. Then another man came forward. He was small, with worried, hooded eyes and TV preacher hair. He wore an olive dress shirt and tie of the kind picked out by a certain kind of wife. He was a white man with a loud whisper.

"Sheriff, we need to deal with this quietly and get this out of the sight of our patrons."

"Everyone here will have to be interviewed before they can leave," Peralta said.

"But that could be two hundred people."

"Everybody," Peralta said. He looked around. "I don't see anybody taking offense. Anyway, it's a tribal and federal case…"

I left them talking and walked ten feet farther.

"So the professor didn't tell the sheriff about his little adventure…"

"Fuck you, Blair." I was all out of devastating one-liners.

Our dustup was threatening to disturb a man who was sitting before a big slot machine called Damnation Alley. The machine was still making sounds of gunfire and action-movie music. It informed us that it could take every kind of bill up to twenty dollars. The man looked frail inside a checked short-sleeve shirt and old blue jeans. Some gamblers are so dedicated they will sit for hours before the slots. It's understandable they might even fall asleep on one. Unfortunately, the small man slumped backward in the seat was merely perfectly balanced by some odd combination of gravity, body mass, and the onset of rigor mortis. When I saw the ice pick handle protruding from his right ear, I'm sure the whole casino could hear the catch in my throat.

Blair watched me. "His wallet's gone. But I met him a while back, with Snyder, when we interviewed him about his brother's body being found in the desert."

"Louis Bell."

# Chapter Thirteen

The small, worried manager conveyed us to an office that overlooked the casino through a darkened, one-way window. I followed Peralta inside and the casino manager went away. The office was large, with a highly polished wood floor, and ornamented with Indian pottery and baskets. A bank of television screens showed different angles of the casino. Out the window, I could see the detectives and crime-scene technicians still gathered around Damnation Alley, as if they expected the corpse of Louis Bell to hit the big payout. If so, it would give the manager yet another reason to worry. Or maybe celebrate. I could imagine the billboards around town: "Casino Arizona, Where You CAN Take It With You." Peralta had moved to the large leather chair behind a long modern desk with a bare top. The chair barely contained his bulk. He just stared at me.

"Well?" I said.

He just shrugged, turning down the corners of his face so he briefly had bulldog jowls. The room was silent. The miniature city of lights out the window gave a sense of the symphony of odds and desperate hopes that lay beyond the thick glass. I walked along the wall, touching the window. The glass was cold. I was cold, and felt fifty pounds heavier from the gathering oppression.

I started talking. "The last time I saw an ice pick used that way was on the Willo home tour. It was stuck in the ear of a man who was lying naked in his bedroom. He owned some check-cashing outlets. Apparently clean—you told me this. Maybe somebody was trying to muscle in, take protection money."

Peralta was swinging slowly in the chair, a heavy pendulum of fate. He said nothing.

"I don't know how that gets us to Louis Bell," I said. "And so ballsy, taking him out in a crowded casino. That's sending a message, right?"

Peralta was looking at the ceiling. I went on, "All I know about Louis is that he honored his brother's last request, to be buried on his own land. This is Arizona, property rights as God and all that. Harry's property was way the hell out beyond the White Tank Mountains. It's good for nothing, unless you want to wait fifty years for Phoenix and LA to grow together. Otherwise, Harry was retired. He lived in a trailer near Hyder. The autopsy came back clean, I guess. So we have two desert rat brothers, and now one gets an ice pick in the ear. I was trying to stay out of this, remember? Follow orders and write a book."

The room was large and without sound again. The floor made weird ghosts of the light coming from recessed positions in the ceiling. I didn't meet his eyes. The bank of television monitors on the other wall got my attention—whoever sat here could watch everything from the blackjack dealer's hands to the parking lot. Maybe one of them would reveal who scrambled Louis Bell's brains. I was growing angry with Peralta for the silent treatment, and at myself for feeling like a kid who was in trouble. What the hell did I do wrong? What was it about his moods that bred paranoia?

"You know about the woman named Dana," I said. "I don't need to go into that again."

I sat on a hard leather loveseat. Maybe the furniture was intended to make whoever sat there uncomfortable, be he employee facing dismissal or unruly customer. I knew the routine. I could feel the anger radiating off him. He didn't like surprises, especially ones that embroiled the Sheriff's Office in other jurisdictions, especially when he might not be able to run the show, as would happen with the feds. Soon he would explode—his rages were always frightening, even if you had lived through a dozen of them, even if you knew the generosity he was capable of in other circumstances. My stomach was tight. My mind was bouncing around the room, down to the slot machines, glancing off the corpse of Louis Bell, and ricocheting back to the glass office. I wondered what Sharon would say. I missed her. They had been married for thirty years, and now she was his "ex-wife." That construction was still foreign. For all the years I knew them it was Mike and Sharon, never just Mike. She had been his awkward young shadow when Peralta and I were first partners. Even then, I like to flatter myself that I could detect a spark, a curiosity. Then she had gone back to school, eventually earning her Ph.D. in psychology. Later she would become the famous radio psychologist, the best-selling author. That seemed like a long time ago. Now she was in San Francisco in a new life. And I was cooped up in this glass cell with her ex-husband.

I said, "It doesn't seem to me that this is our problem. The guy in Willo is a Phoenix PD case. This one is tribal cops and the FBI…"

I was talking to myself. Talking myself out of the obvious. All the ways human beings hurt each other in Maricopa County, Arizona, and I'm just the egghead who paws through the old records, clears out the old cases. So what if I'm bracketed by homicide by ice picks. What's the connection between Alan Cordesman, check-cashing king, and Louis Bell, old fart at the casino? Not my problem. Murder in the next block of my neighborhood? It can happen anywhere. Same MO used for the brother of a dead man I discovered courtesy of my mysterious former student? Coincidence. Hell, maybe it was the new killing method being shown in gangsta videos or wherever the pathologies of our civilization are passed on today. It wasn't my problem. Unfortunately, that's not what the worry pain in my middle told me.

Out of a dry mouth I said, "I need to find this woman, Dana. She's a connection somehow."

"I agree," he said evenly. He stopped swinging in the chair.

I stared at him. "You agree? What about me being chained to your book, trying to be a real historian—I think that's how you put it—not being a hot dog, and not interfering with a PPD investigation?"

His large eyes filled with innocent surprise. "Why are you so upset, Mapstone…?"

Movement drew our eyes to the big window. The crowd surged like disturbed water, and we saw several uniformed officers pushing through. They appeared to be chasing someone. I looked at Peralta, but he was already halfway to the door. We walked quickly down the steps. Getting across the casino floor was easy by following in the jetstream of Peralta. Then we burst out the door into the blinding sunshine. Four tribal cops were handcuffing a slight Hispanic kid. He couldn't have been more than twenty, with a razor cut and dramatic thick eyebrows. He had that odd look of the newly arrested, part confusion and part defiance. One of the tribal cops explained what had happened.

"He tried to make a run for it, and when we caught him he had this in his pocket."

Peralta pulled out a handkerchief and took the wallet, then carefully opened it.

He said, "Driver's license says Louis Bell."

# Chapter Fourteen

I had my plan for that evening. Mexican food with Lindsey at Los Dos Molinos and then some reconnect time at home. The restaurant sat near the foot of the South Mountains in a building that was once Tom Mix's house. And even though the cowboy star was long gone, the place was the best in town for the kind of New Mexico-style cuisine that is so spicy it makes you sweat. Even with the tourists fleeing the impending summer, Los Dos was crowded. The hostess was so unbending I'm convinced even Peralta couldn't just walk in and get a table. So, after putting our name on the waiting list, we did the usual penance with the crowd on the patio, eased by beer and chips.

"So he was killed while playing slots?" Lindsey kept her voice down and her eyes wide with interest. "Talk about hitting God's jackpot."

"Or not," I said. "Catching the suspect with the victim's wallet in front of a hundred witnesses ought to be enough that even Patrick Blair could get a conviction."

"Dave," she laughed. "What has he ever done to you?"

Part of me would have loved to ask. Ask, that is, what has he ever done to Lindsey? Part of me cowered in primitive emotions and another part was alive with aroused voyeurism. How odd: to have lived a life of the mind; that life was supposed to tame and mediate those nasty feelings, take them out and study them, make them safe, even boring. Mountbatten, the last British viceroy in India, was cuckolded by Nehru—that gave the historians a laugh. And it wasn't as if I hadn't enjoyed enough romantic adventures to make up for my youthful awkwardness. Then I won the great prize that sat across from me, sipping her Modelo Especial and dipping a chip into the hottest salsa. So I didn't ask…and I didn't tell, either, about Gretchen. Lindsey said she didn't want to know that much about my old lovers, that it was better for her mental health. She was wise as always.

"Professor…" she said, squeezing my hand. "You have that faraway look."

I smiled at her. Her dark hair shone lustrously in the dimness. It brushed her collar when she moved her head.

I said, "Tell me about your day."

"Just computer stuff," she said. "Still helping our good friends at the Justice Department."

"You are such a big deal."

"To you. And I'm glad of that. It kind of scares me what we can do now—how little privacy people have, and they don't even know it. But it scares me that bad guys like terrorists can hide their money in cyberspace and move it with the touch of a finger. So…"

She let the words trail off. Inside the cantina, I could hear the third rendition of "Hotel California" by the guitarist. He had drunken accompaniment from some patrons.

Lindsey went on, "Robin thinks what we do is a threat to civil liberties. I never thought of it that way. But maybe she's right."

"How is she doing? Peralta wants to know."

"Really? Peralta courting my sister. That's too weird to contemplate." She made a face. "I think she'd be a handful for any man, so I'm glad she's got this Edward. Although I'd like to meet him. Why do you think she hasn't introduced us to him? Am I being a typical big sister?"

I shook my head, nodded. She laughed. My insides were so relieved that our spat of the morning was forgotten.

"I don't know how to be a normal sister," she said. "I don't know what that's like. Maybe there's no such thing. But the training sure wouldn't have come from my family. Sometimes I can't figure Robin out. We'll be going along, and something I say will set her off. She can be very emotional. We had a fight yesterday where she essentially blamed me for Linda killing herself. Then it was over and she apologized and we made up. It can be a rollercoaster." She brushed back an errant strand of hair. "I heard a radio report the other day…I kind of half heard it. But some expert was talking about how relationships are like physics, and if you're really into somebody you feel everything—love, hate, fear. It made me think, at least. So if I seemed like a bitch this morning, I'm so sorry, Dave."

"No, no," I said. "I was out of line. I'm being too hard on Robin."

"She likes you, Dave. She thinks you're very smart and attractive."

I was going to speak, but then the loudspeaker called our name and we went toward the cantina. Another round of "Hotel California" was starting up.

By the time we paid our bill and headed for the parking lot, it was closing in on eleven o'clock. But instead of turning north on Central toward the city, Lindsey steered to the right.

"What?"

"You'll find out."

Now it was clear that Lindsey had her plan for the evening, too. She turned on Dobbins and avoided the closed entrance to the park. We headed east past houses that hadn't been there when I was a kid—that statement could be my standard disclaimer about virtually any Arizona vista. Then the park came closer to the road. Lindsey pulled off the road and gave me a long, luxurious kiss.

She pointed to a sleeping bag in the back seat. "You could carry that."

"The park closed at sunset," I mumbled.

"So call the police."

Our walk was lit by stars and city lights. They made the barrel cactuses and boulders into shadowy companions as we picked our way up a steady incline. Critters scampered away with snaps and rustles as we walked. I wanted to think they were all jackrabbits and roadrunners. But the landscape seemed benign. The night was as dry as an old manuscript, with the desert air offering no resistance to our hike. She gave me her hand and I helped her across a break in the rocks. Ahead of us were the low mountains that are a fixture in the Phoenix landscape. Lost? Check your directions by the mountains. But from where we stood, they presented themselves as a steady black uplift that suddenly cut off leaving nothing but sky. Our navigation stars came from the television towers above the Dobbins Overlook, dozens of red lights blinking reassuringly. I had hiked these trails many times as a Cub Scout, but was ashamed to say I hadn't been back since I returned home to Phoenix as an adult. But I wasn't feeling like a Cub Scout right that moment.

Lindsey took the sleeping bag out of my hand and deposited it on the ground. We stood on a sandy, flat pause in the earth, surrounded by saguaros and rocks the size of sentinels. Above us, the torrid red stars pulsed and below us Phoenix spread out like a galaxy turned on its side. We just watched the lights, saying nothing. I slipped my hand around her waist, a feeling so wonderfully familiar—so right—and yet still so novel. The only sound was the everywhere-and-nowhere roar of the city below us. Then she was unbuttoning my shirt.

All the stars were still glowing later. Lindsey lay back against me. I nuzzled her neck and draped an arm over her breasts. Her fair skin was my oasis amid the blackness of the desert at night.

"Tell me a story, History Shamus."

"South Mountain Park is the largest municipal park in the world. The only historic murder I know of happened in…"

She shook her head. "Tell me a hopeful story."

I pushed my nose through her soft hair and nibbled her ear. She laughed her low, adult laugh. The horizon of lights blinked insistently. Amid the lights, the night was clear enough to make out Camelback Mountain miles to the north.

"This place lay abandoned for four hundred years," I said, "except for the ghosts of its past and the phantasms of its possibilities. Here was one of the most fertile river valleys in the world. A Nile or a Euphrates. And yet, if you had ridden your horse into it in 1870, you would have found it empty."

"I like this story," she said.

"It's called Phoenix because it rose from its ashes, like the bird of mythology. The ashes were the Hohokam, who built one of the most advanced irrigation societies in the New World. But the river was capricious—flooding in the spring, but then going years with barely a trickle. The Hohokam civilization disappeared—what happened is still a mystery. Then after the Civil War, settlers found this place and cleared out the old Indian canals. They were on the verge of abandoning it, too. But they dreamed what it could be. And mighty acts of faith and technology made the desert bloom. Now it's the fifth-largest city in the nation."

She leaned her head back and kissed me.

"You're a romantic," she said.

I adjusted myself so I could feel the length of her back against my chest. I said, "When I was a kid, the city was surrounded by fields and citrus groves. From up here in the daytime, we could have looked down and seen orange trees, then the Japanese flower gardens—they seemed to go on forever. Then, the city. It was beautiful. Too bad we had to pave it all over."

"I wish I could have seen it, History Shamus. I just don't know why we have to lose so much that's beautiful."

It was after one a.m. when we turned down Cypress Street. My body was feeling worked out and giddy in a way that comes from only one source. I was already imagining curling up in bed with my lover. But someone was on the porch, sitting on the step.

"What is Robin doing here," Lindsey said sleepily. Then, in a tense voice, "My God, look at her eye."

# Chapter Fifteen

The city kept growing. Mile-long trains brought lumber and steel that soon became buildings. Eternal desert turned into ephemeral subdivisions, offices and retail strips. Sixteen billion dollars in new highways. Four thousand new construction jobs a month. From mountain reservoirs and a canal from the Colorado River came 400 billion gallons of water a year to support a megalopolis in a place that received a mere seven inches of rain a year. The growth leapt over mountain ranges and rerouted rivers. It inspired new policy centers at the university and lively debates in the newspaper. You heard it in the rhythm of heavy equipment and nail guns, and the music of melodious Spanish spoken by the framing crews in a hundred developments. You saw it in the ubiquitous pickup trucks of contractors and tradesmen, lined up in traffic on the freeways and ornamenting subdivision driveways. As May turned into June and the temperature shot above one hundred ten, I was reminded that our summers were getting longer and hotter. But hardly anyone in Phoenix had been around long enough to know this.

Robin moved in with us, staying in the small apartment over the garage that connected to the main house by the walkway that led off the living room. You got to it by taking the bookcase-backed stairway on the north end of the living room. The arrangement had been my suggestion, made after a very long night when we had found her battered and waiting for us on the front step. She had had a fight with her boyfriend, the elusive Edward. The damage to Robin was a nasty purple splotch growing around her left eye. Lindsey had immediately wanted to call the police. Then she was ready to arrest him herself. I had never seen my wife so depart from the preternatural calm that is so much a part of her. At one point, Robin was physically holding Lindsey back from the phone or the door. Robin said she, too, was to blame, and had given as good as she got in the fight. She just wanted to get away from Edward and let the relationship be over.

Lindsey, who had seen plenty of domestic violence as a young deputy, would have none of it. "The woman always blames herself," she said. "This asshole will do it again, if not with you then with someone else." And then: "You know this happened to Linda more than once. We watched it happen, remember?"

I felt out of my element, watching these two women who, until a few months ago, hadn't seen each other in years and yet were connected by invisible strings of blood and personal history. I fetched ice for Robin, and mostly kept my mouth shut. There are times to not take charge. Finally, though, I broke the stalemate. Robin would stay with us for a few days. I offered to go with her the next day to retrieve her things from Edward's house. But she refused help, saying that he was leaving on a business trip and the next day it would be safe for her to go alone. Lindsey never wavered from wanting to arrest and prosecute the bastard, as she unfailingly referred to him.

Two weeks later, Robin was still in the little apartment that had served, at various times, as Grandmother's sewing room and Grandfather's office. Nobody seemed to mind the arrangement. Lindsey was on loan to the Justice Department, so she left early for the federal building downtown. Some days I worked at home, and this gave me my first one-on-one conversations with my sister-in-law. She talked a lot, much of it about herself. But just when it risked becoming tedious, she was suddenly very interested in me, in my experiences and opinions.

Sometimes, I thought she was testing me.

"Lindsey's gained weight," she pronounced one day.

"I think she's beautiful," I said.

"I hadn't seen her in years," she said. "Anyway, maybe it's because she's happy."

Other times, I began to see her inner turbulence. One morning we started talking about a college education, but by the end Robin was nearly shrieking at me about how she'd had to go to work when she was fourteen and I was being a snob. She had attended the University of Delaware, so I don't know where she got the impression I was looking down on her. Later she apologized. But we had other talks that took the same course—not many, but once in a while. I came to realize that Robin had a very different emotional arc from Lindsey.

Robin was a major jock and enjoyed running through Willo. When I was home, she would stop in the study after her run to talk. I would get close to heat exhaustion from the two-block walk to the bus stop. She merely displayed a healthy glisten of sweat and breathed as easy as if she were sleeping. In her running togs, she was quite a specimen: tanned, muscled, and leonine with her thick, long hair. She was leggy like Lindsey, but her calves and quads were well defined. Her breasts were larger. This was all women-in-the-abstract, a condition that comes from a satisfying marriage to the woman you find most attractive in the world. And even in my hungriest horn-dog days, I wouldn't have let myself contemplate my wife's sister. And she still had that cute boy's face.

"Lindsey Faith was always the pretty one," she said as if reading my thoughts. "I think I look more like my dad. She has Linda's beauty. But I'd say she's luckier in love. I hope so, David. Don't take that the wrong way, I'm just kind of down on all relationships right now."

I said I could understand.

"The old me would really hate Lindsey for what she has. With you, the house, the whole domestic bliss routine." She winked at me. "But that's the old me. Lindsey told me you lost your folks when you were a baby. And you don't have any brothers or sisters."

She looked away and said, "I always felt alone, too."

I had my own distraction: finding Dana. In this, I couldn't have been worse off. I had no name I was certain of. No date of birth. No Social Security Number. These were the essentials for taking advantage of the vast and growing tentacles of law enforcement. I had no photo—just her story, a lie no doubt, and the memory of her face and manner, flawed I am sure. Eyewitness accounts are often so. When I was a patrol deputy, we called them "eye-witless"—fifty people can see the same event and each could have a different and conflicting recollection. That was proving true in the investigation of the ice-pick murder of Louis Bell. The medical examiner fixed the time of death at around eleven that morning, and for two hours he sat slumped into the chair where he was finally discovered. Still, there had been around two hundred fifty people in the casino. All had been interviewed by the cops, and nobody remembered seeing anything. He might have gone undiscovered for hours longer had not a grandmother from Sun City been antsy to play the slot machine he was blocking.

But we had a suspect anyway. His name was Jesus Esparza, age eighteen, a small-time hood with burglary, pickpocket, and prostitution arrests. The feds liked him for the murder, and Phoenix PD was looking to connect him to the Cordesman murder. That one might be trickier, considering there was no forced entry and apparently nothing missing. This brought Peralta back to his first theory. Maybe Esparza was a hustler that Cordesman had picked up and taken home. Cordesman was single, and the neighbors didn't recall seeing any women come and go from the house. I was more skeptical. I couldn't set aside the visit from my former student to send me on a fool's errand in the desert, one that had led me to one body, to the Bell brothers, and finally to Louis Bell with an ice pick in his brain.

I was down to calling every person named Underwood and Watkins in the phone book. This yielded nothing but ill will for the Sheriff's Office, as if I were just another telemarketer. I could bet I was on the verge of ill will from the sheriff himself, every day that I didn't produce the soccer mom with the letter from dear old dad. The second Monday in June, I drove out to a construction site in Maricopa, following my last lead. Just a few years before, this village stood as an isolated dust-catcher on the other side of the South Mountains. Its momentary importance had come a century before, when it was the connection to the railroad from Phoenix. But as I drove out the long, two-lane highway, I could see how much had changed. Subdivisions rose on both sides of the road, completed houses or framing, behind mud-colored walls. The combination of the dun-colored, flat land and monotonous new housing was numbing. The "yards" in front of each house were not even large enough to plant one tree. I didn't get the appeal. But part of it must have come from signs promising prices in the high ninety-thousands, well below Phoenix proper.

My destination was an uninspiring expanse of desert, where I found a man sitting in a new Mercedes convertible. He got out and introduced himself as Josh.

"Hope my directions were good, Deputy Mapstone," he said, pronouncing it like "Map-stun." "I'm all over the Valley in my job, so I appreciate you working around that." He had a pale, round face and shaved head. Although he wore expensive-looking slacks, he topped them off with a T-shirt. It showed an image of the planet and the caption: "Seventy percent of the Earth's surface is water. The rest is available."

"Sure," I said. "What exactly do you do?"

"I assemble land," he said. He was a fast talker. "Me and my partners. This here," he poked his thumb at the desert, "this will eventually be five thousand homes. But first we have to put together the deal for the developers. A property this size might come from twenty or thirty different purchases of land. Some of them are just a few acres; maybe a family's held it for generations. The trick is to get these farmers to sell."

"Is it hard?"

"Nah," he said. "But they keep wanting more money."

"I saw your name in the Miami alumni newsletter," I said. "You contributed an item about an alum who had received a community award here."

"Yeah, Ted Griffin. You must do some obscure reading," he said, slower now.

"I wondered if you might be in touch with people here who attended Miami?"

"Not really," he said. "A few. You can't swing a dead cat in Phoenix without hitting somebody from Ohio."

I told him who I was after, and he shook his head faster with each specific detail of Dana's description. Hell, I knew I was playing long hunches, but they were all I had left. In a few minutes, I left him with his Mercedes and his empty land, and I began the long, depressing drive back to the city. To make matters worse, the old county Crown Vic only had an AM radio, so I absently pushed buttons to take me from commercial-filled rock stations to commercial-filled country stations. I almost didn't hear it.

"Arizona Dreams," the voice said. "Your home town. Imagine a master-planned community that's a real community, with real neighborhoods, like you remember from when you were a kid. We're imagining that for you, at Arizona Dreams…"

The sales pitch was droning on long after I had slammed on the brakes and pulled off next to a cotton field. The only thing I was buying was the voice. That pleasant voice with a hint of butterscotch.

I said out loud, "Hello, Dana."

# Chapter Sixteen

Two days later, I borrowed Lindsey's Prelude, put Coleman Hawkins in the CD player and got on the freeway. Even though I played "Father Cooperates" twice, it occurred to me how out of place the music was for Phoenix suburban commuting. This was music for city sidewalks and basement jazz clubs, for smoky introspection. It didn't blur your mind, like country or hip-hop. Hawkins made you want to be right there, listening to every note. He was out of place here, like me. I went east on the Red Mountain Freeway, trying to beat the afternoon rush hour. It was only two o'clock. But I hit traffic by the time I came to Tempe, and it never let up. One of the perverse outcomes of years of a building mania on the city fringes was that the supposedly quiet suburbs suffered from monstrous congestion. Things got worse when I came to the Price Freeway and turned south.

In another thirty minutes, I landed in Gilbert. For a few minutes, I just drove around, getting my bearings. When I was in college, this had been a tiny farm town surrounded by fields, far from the nearest inkling of city. Now it was dense with red tile roofs, that tedious signature of the Phoenix building industry. I drove past subdivisions with names like Summer Meadows, Neely Ranch, and Madera Parc. I wondered if that "c" on "parc" let the developer add another ten percent to the price. And there probably once had been a Neely Ranch, a real ranch. But all I saw now were houses jammed together on the flat former farmland.

I looked down side streets: the fronts of the stucco houses were mostly garage doors, all the same paint scheme, no trees. And yet families were clamoring to get to Gilbert, if the newspaper was to be believed. The East Valley cities of Gilbert, Chandler, and Queen Creek, along with the Ahwatukee section of Phoenix, had become the white, upper-middle-class promised land of the Valley. There were two geographies of the mind here. For me, I looked around and saw all that was lost: citrus groves and flower gardens, clean air and a sweeter town. But for the newcomers, and almost everyone was, this was clean and new and warm. They had the good schools, youth sports, chain stores, and long drives that characterized the upper-income American suburban life. That, and they didn't see anyone with brown or black skin or anyone who was poor.

It was an unsettling geography. Neighborhoods didn't connect to anything. Neighborhoods segregated by "price point." Each was walled off from the world. The main roads were seven or eight lanes wide, separated from everything else by wide berms and landscaped dead zones. The buildings were all brand new, but sterile. At the dawn of the twentieth century, architects like Daniel Burnham had sought to create lovely and humane civic design. So was born the City Beautiful Movement. Now our newly built spaces were all about maximum profit. They were spaces of convenience and automobiles and yet at the human level they were spaces for prosaic drudgery. The City Beautiful streets of Willo and central Phoenix might as well have been a world away.

And yet, I came upon a little town embedded in all this new suburbia. It was poignantly out of place, with its humble ranch houses with their low roofs. Once fields had surrounded them; now it was fields of houses. I crossed the Consolidated Canal and pulled into the Mormon Church parking lot to check my map. Finding Dana hadn't been easy. But I called in a favor from a radio producer I knew, and she supplied a phone number for the woman who did the Arizona Dreams ad. Then I cross-referenced the number for the address.

Dana's house was located in a nicer part of town. Here the subdivisions were named Lakeside, Crystal Shores, and Regatta, and the houses were blessed with a rolling landscape, lush grass, older trees, and shade. A road took me over a bridge where I could see the lake that backed up to the houses. Some sizable boats were tied up. It looked like a synthetic reproduction of a Florida or California development. Those were fake, but at least they could spare the water. This was also "gated community" territory. But a landscape truck was helpfully sitting across the open gate into the subdivision I was seeking, so I just drove through. Why, they'll let anybody come in.

The house looked like every other one on the street, aside from a subtle rearrangement of some stonework or shade of tan paint. The architecture was like a mutt dog: watered-down Spanish colonial, pre-fab Tuscany, and a pinch of the homelier aspects of Tudor. There were three narrow arched windows facing the street, mounted in stucco and stonework, but somehow they didn't seem to go with the rest of the front. A good half of the part that faced the street was a garage door. That meant most of the front yard was driveway, in this case an elaborate mix of brick and stone. What was left had been given over to a tiny lawn, unnaturally green, surrounded by beds of rocks and desert xeriscape plants. I was no architect, but let's just say it was a long way from Willo.

The doorbell set off a choir of dogs. I stood off to the side—it was a habit from my patrol days, when a knock might be met with gunfire through the door, and it also made sure she couldn't see me through the peephole. There was no car in the driveway. But if she wasn't home from work, I was willing to wait. Reiterating that willingness was about the time it took for the door to be pulled open. It was the strawberry-blonde mom from my office, and she had a merry greeting smile on her face. That is, until she saw me. She stepped back quickly and pushed at the door, but I was ready for that. I pushed back hard, sending the door into the wall and her back toward the dogs. They were two Rottweilers, and they didn't like me one bit.

"Get control of those dogs now or I'll shoot them," I said above the barking, forcing my voice down as I felt a giant pool of sweat form on my back. I put my hand on the butt of the Colt Python .357 Magnum holstered on my belt. But I didn't retreat out of the doorjamb.

"No, no!" Dana said quickly. "I'll put them away. Come on, Precious, come on, Brownie." She pulled Precious and Brownie away with difficulty and dragged them down a hallway. I gradually took my hand off the butt of the pistol and surveyed the foyer. Everything looked expensive and impersonal, as if bought whole from displays at Scottsdale stores. Then she reappeared and walked quickly toward me, and then we were outside. She closed the door behind her.

"What are you doing here?" she said, all the butterscotch gone from her voice. "You can't be here! I've got to go pick up Madison from band practice!" I didn't budge.

She grimaced. "My husband might be home any minute."

"We'll bring him into the conversation, too," I said.

"You don't understand," she said, taking me by the arm and starting to walk toward the car. I stayed put. She had a wild look. "Do you have any idea who my husband is?"

"Considering you lied about who you are, no."

"He's Tom Earley."

At first it didn't sink in. I shrugged my shoulders and started to speak.

She cut me off. "County Supervisor Tom Earley." She said it emphasizing every syllable.

I drew in a breath and looked at her. This was the guy who had been questioning my job to Peralta. I felt a strange caution shiver from my spine up into my brain. I set it aside.

I said, "So? That's not my problem. Sheriff Peralta has put politicians in jail before. And he has nice facilities for their wives, too."

I thought she was going to faint. "Mapstone," she stuttered, "I can't...I didn't..."

"You did," I said. "You filed a false report. That's against the law."

"But I…" She grabbed my arm again, her eyes glistening in near-tears. "Please give me a chance to explain."

"I am. Invite me inside. We can have a nice long talk. Reminisce about the days at Miami. That beautiful campus in Oxford. What a great teacher I was."

She shook her head vehemently. "I cannot let Tom find you here! Please…meet me tomorrow. I promise I'll tell you everything. Please!"

I was ready to be a hardass, but something in her plea softened me. I'm a patsy. So we agreed on a time and place for the next day. I told her I would be back on her doorstep with uniformed deputies if she failed to show up. Even inside my car, I could still hear the dogs barking.

I drove back downtown on the Price Freeway, watching the hardening of the traffic arteries going in the other direction. What a lifestyle. Out to the suburbs. Out to safety. That was the theory, at least. Yet the paper that morning told of a girl being abducted and raped not a half mile from the walled subdivision I had just left. And the running gunbattle down Chandler Boulevard the night before. A fourteen-year-old girl had guns at home and a plan to shoot up her school in Gilbert. And the armored-car guard gunned down in Ahwatukee. So no place was safe. Which was good for job security in law enforcement, unless you were the freak with the Ph.D. in history who was a patsy for wives with excuses. Somewhere in the gridlock, County Supervisor Tom Earley was headed back to his lifestyle, and his Dana with secrets. I wondered if he still wanted to X me out of the sheriff's budget. He probably would really want to now. I was on the way home to Lindsey and a martini, a much preferable destination.

# Chapter Seventeen

Business was strong at the Home Depot on Grand Avenue. That was true, at least, on the curb at the edge of the parking lot, where the independent contractors that comprised Phoenix's piece of the global economy did what they could. They were lean brown men in jeans, with ball caps and cowboy hats, their number fluctuating around a dozen depending on the traffic. I watched as a Ford pickup stopped, engaged in a curbside negotiation. Three men then jumped in the truck bed and it drove off to whatever construction or landscaping work was to be done. I wondered what was the going rate? Five bucks an hour? A tidy fortune compared to the men's poor villages in the interior of Mexico or Central America. Dana watched me watching the commerce.

"They should send them all back to Mexico," she said primly. "That's what my husband says."

"That will be a neat trick," I said, "considering there are probably half a million illegals in just a few miles around us."

Dana looked at me with alarm.

"They won't hurt you," I said. "Anyway, how would you be able to buy so much house for the money without illegal immigrant labor."

"You're such a cynic, David," she said. "I keep wanting to call you Dr. Mapstone."

We were sitting inside her gray SUV. It was called an Armada, and seemed at least two stories above ground and suitably armored to protect us from the Home Depot parking lot. We were far from Gilbert, hard by the railroad tracks and the ever expanding west side barrio, far enough for Dana to feel safe meeting me. I said, "I don't care what you call me. We're not friends. You're lucky I didn't arrest you yesterday."

Her face flushed further, a neat trick. It started to match the scarlet blouse she was wearing.

"I really was at Miami," she said. "And you really were my teacher."

"What year?" I demanded.

"Nineteen eighty-five."

"Where did class meet?"

"The room? I don't know. Somewhere in Upham Hall."

I watched her carefully, but she stared straight ahead, avoiding my glare. She added, "I had quite a crush on you."

"You're still lying."

"I didn't lie!" she said, her voice rising. She scolded me as if I were one of her kids running the television too loud. "You found a body, didn't you? Right where the note said."

"The man in the desert was killed by your father?"

"That's what the note said!"

I explained that Harry Bell's body had only been in the desert a few weeks, not since the mid-1960s. I wondered if I would be so patient if her husband weren't a county supervisor. She stared so hard at the windshield her eyes might have popped out and made a run for it. Then she started sniffling and tears beat her eyes to the exit.

"Try again," I said.

"Bastard!"

"You had a crush on me, remember?"

We sat in silence, the only sound being the quiet purr of the engine and the air conditioning. Outside, the temperature was climbing above a hundred. Soon it would be hot enough to make all the new transplants wonder what the hell they were thinking when they decided to move here. Inside, I was uneasy. The more I had thought about Dana and Tom Earley—"stewed about it," as Lindsey would say—the more I worried that I was being used to embarrass the sheriff. It made sense: this persistent critic of the Sheriff's Office, and me in particular, had sent his wife to concoct a historic case. Then Mapstone would waste sheriff's resources digging up a man who had died of natural causes and only wanted to be buried on his own land. Why the hell was I sitting here? I should have been alerting Peralta. But if this was the game, why hadn't the trap been sprung back in February when we discovered the body?

My misgivings were interrupted by the sound of sobs. Dana was bent forward with her face in her hands.

"It's my fault," she said. "It's my fault."

"What is your fault?" I asked.

"This," she said. "Misleading you. There was no real letter from my father. He's alive and living in Gold Canyon. I needed help. I didn't know where to turn."

I kept quiet.

"Back in the late eighties, my husband was a partner with two vile little men, Harry and Louis Bell. Tom was just building his real-estate business, and the Bells owned some land in Tempe. We developed a little shopping center. There was lots of savings and loan money then, so everybody was doing something."

As her tears subsided, she talked straight-ahead and business-like. Gone was the elliptical ditziness that she had shown in my office, whether it was an act or not.

"The Bells swindled us," she continued. "It was a complicated case, so I won't bore you with the details. We took them to court, and won. But they filed for bankruptcy, and we never got a dime."

I settled back in my seat and said nothing. Across the parking lot, business had slowed down. The men milled about like a meaningless picket line. The combination of heat and exhaust fumes in the air gave them an insubstantial, ghostly look.

"Well," she went on, "about two years ago, I started getting phone calls. It was a man, he didn't give his name, He always called when Tom was gone. He said he had information that we had broken the law on the shopping center investment, and he asked for money to keep quiet about it."

"Who was this?"

"I'm not sure," she said. "I always thought it must be Harry Bell. Tom was very successful and well-known by then. So Harry was going to get revenge for being forced into bankruptcy."

"Why not go to the police?"

Dana stared straight ahead. She kept running her finger along her seat belt shoulder strap like a barber sharpening a straight razor.

I said, "So Bell had something on you and your husband."

"Look, it was a long time ago," she said. Now her hand clutched the shoulder strap. "This man said he could prove that Tom had defrauded his partners and the RTC in the shopping center deal. Well, those were the Bell brothers. He claimed he had documents. He said he would go to the media."

"Did he defraud them?"

"Of course not!" she said.

"So why not go to the cops?"

"You don't understand," she said. "My husband is a great man. He has so much to give. I couldn't let them hurt him this way. I never even told him about the calls. So I agreed to pay. I had inherited some money a few years back from my aunt. Ten thousand dollars. It seemed worth it to protect Tom. It was just like a movie. I took out the money as one-hundred-dollar bills, and put them in a gym bag. He told me to take the bag to Superstition Springs Mall and leave it behind this certain palm tree in the south parking lot. And I did. Three days later I got the documents in the mail."

I was sweating despite the air conditioning going full blast. I said, "I still don't believe you. Want to try another lie?"

"This is the truth," she said quietly.

"The calls stopped after I paid," she went on. "For a while. Then, after the first of the year, they started again. This time the man said he knew my husband had killed Harry Bell. It just sounded mad. But I looked in the newspaper to see if there was a death notice, and there was. It didn't say much. There was no word about how he died. Then one Saturday, a letter comes in the mail. It has a photo of this rocky grave in the desert and instructions on how to get there. Thank God, Tom wasn't home to see this. There was a note. It said I was to pay $100,000 or he would go to the police with evidence that Tom had killed Harry Bell and put him out there. So I came to you." She stared at me and her large green eyes looked liquid—with tears, emotion, acting, I couldn't tell.

"This doesn't make any sense," I said. "Why would you come to me? How did you even know about me?"

"I really was in your class, David," she said, touching my hand. I drew it back. "You don't even remember me."

I couldn't recall her at all. I wondered if I was lost in the fog of a brain in its forties, or if I were being played as a patsy.

I said, "So why not tell me the truth? Why lie?"

"I had to protect Tom," she said, her eyes closed tightly. "He has enemies, you see. Any great man does. If I had gone to the real police, and told them I had paid blackmail money—it would have been all over the newspaper."

"So instead of the real police, you came to the play police—me."

"Please." She touched my hand again. "Don't be offended. I thought if I gave you a trail, you'd follow it and get these people who were doing this to us. I read the papers and watch TV. I know some of the big cases you've cracked. So I gave you the story that I did. If a man had been murdered and buried out there, you could get to the bottom of it. And it obviously worked. I haven't gotten another letter or phone call."

I angled myself to face her and moved in close. I didn't want her to have a chance to look away.

"There's just one problem," I said. "If you suspected the Bell brothers of blackmailing you, then you had a perfect motive for murdering Louis Bell."

Her eyes widened and she swallowed with difficulty. "What are you saying?" she rasped.

"Louis Bell was murdered last week. Somebody stuck an ice pick in his brain."

She shook her head and said nothing.

"Do you know the name Alan Cordesman?" I demanded.

"No! What do you want from me?"

"The truth."

"I am telling you the truth!" she screamed.

We just stared at each other. The men across the parking lot were sitting down now, letting the sun beat on them. I opened the door and dropped to the pavement.

"You'd better get me that blackmail note with the photo of the grave," I said. "Or I will go to the sheriff, and I don't care who your husband is."

I looked back at Dana. She was red-faced, puffy-eyed and about to say something. But I slammed the door and walked away.

# Chapter Eighteen

I tried to sort it out that afternoon with Lindsey. She had stopped by my office after lunch, looking like a million bucks in a black pantsuit.

"Maybe this woman is just nuts," she said, sitting on my desk, facing me, while I rubbed her feet.

"Mmmm," she said.

"Is that irritating you?"

"I'll bear up," she said. "I'll tell you when to stop."

I said, "Peralta says I'm the one who's nuts. He was as angry as I've ever seen him that I had anything to do with Tom Earley's wife. He didn't want any explanations. He just ordered me to stay away. Why is he so afraid of Tom Earley?"

"Earley wants to destroy El Jefe," she said. "He and his allies call the sheriff a liberal. Can you believe that?"

I shook my head. "Politics have become so extreme, especially in Arizona. When I was a professor, I was considered right-wing. In today's Arizona, I'm what the Tom Earleys of the state would call a liberal, or a socialist." I sighed. "Considering Earley was specifically questioning the need for me in the Sheriff's Office, I should be the one who's scared. I know Peralta's just looking out for me. But the whole thing is creepy. Tom Earley uses me as political cannon fodder, and his wife shows up in my office. If Dana's story is true, and she was a blackmail victim, she wouldn't be a cooperative witness. She's got to protect her husband."

"Maybe she's protecting herself," Lindsey said.

I gently caressed her finely sculpted ankles. I could see why the Victorians thought the sight of a woman's ankle was a scandal.

"I just need to get out of it," I said. "Pass this information on to the detectives. Let them sort it out. I told Peralta I'd find her, and I did." I started on the other foot. "Or," I said, "I could ignore Peralta and arrest her for filing a false report."

"Don't get in a fight with the East Valley, Dave," she laughed. "That would hurt El Jefe's reelection chances."

"That whole suburban thing baffles me," I said.

"It's not your thing, Dave. Not mine, either. Why don't you just give it to the detectives and go back to the book."

"Peralta's book," I said.

"It's my History Shamus' book," she said, smiling at me warmly. "I love the parts you've read to me. I lived some of those cases with you. Anyway, you've seemed contented when you're writing. I like that."

She leaned forward and ran her fingers through my hair. "But there's bad news."

"I'm going bald?"

"No, Dave. I do love your wavy hair, and it's fine. But I just came from the federal building, and they want me in Washington for a week. There was a major breach of corporate computer systems yesterday. Cisco, Bank of America, a bunch of others. Who knows what the hackers got away with."

"You'll have fun," I said, without enthusiasm.

"I'd have fun on vacation there with you, whispering history in my ear as we toured the city. Instead, I'll be cooped up at the FBI in endless meetings with a bunch of propeller-heads. I hate to leave My Love. But when I get back, we get to leave on our real vacation. It's going to be wonderful, Dave!"

She made me smile. "I am so looking forward to that, especially the time with you." I kissed her hand. "In the meantime, I'll be fine. Don't be gone long."

She put her hand on my cheek, looking at me with her dark blue eyes. "I need you, Dave. You keep me centered."

I leaned up and kissed her, letting our tongues dance together. "I'm so proud of you," I said. "Please be safe. Remember the Russian mafia…"

She sat back. "I think about it all the time," she said. "Maybe we should make that life change we talked about. We could make some money off the house. Go someplace that's not so screwed up, get real jobs."

"We would have done that if I hadn't failed in Portland," I said.

"You didn't fail. They were assholes who didn't see how brilliant you are." Then, "I hope it's not a problem that Robin is still at the house."

"I hardly see her," I said. "It's not a problem at all. Maybe I'll take her to dinner with Peralta, be a chaperone."

"He does like her," Lindsey said. "She said today that I was a bitch."

I just watched her. I reached above the fabric of her pants and massaged her calf.

"It's a sister thing," she said, running her hand through her hair. "Seriously, Dave. I know she's kind of like the houseguest that won't leave. But she's been through a bad experience, and I haven't wanted to nag her."

"It's not a problem."

"I won't be gone long, Dave. Just a week."

"I know," I said. "I'll just be writing. Everybody can sleep better knowing they got the ice-pick killer. If they got him."

She raised an eyebrow.

I said, "I could see Patrick Blair using a Taser on the poor guy's nuts to get a confession."

Lindsey just looked at me. Then she withdrew her leg.

Something had changed in the big room. I said, "I was making a joke."

"Patrick is very professional and kind," she said quietly. "He wouldn't do that."

"It was a joke, Lindsey," I said, feeling my face flush. "I'm sorry I offended your friend. I'm glad he has you to defend him." My voice had an edge to it. I could hear that.

"What is it about you and Patrick?"

Before I could answer, she added quickly, "I know you're after some trip to the dark side. I don't know why."

I stammered, "I was just joking."

"No you weren't."

The office air was filled with static electricity of things unsaid, unasked. A long time passed in silence. Then Lindsey touched my hand lightly and left. She didn't slam the door.

# Chapter Nineteen

The next night was a Friday. The sunset took over the entire sky, starting with a subtle pink in the east, then turning to ever more lurid oranges and crimsons in the west. The colors spread out across ripples of high thin clouds that seemed drawn by gravity into chasing the end of the day. If you haven't seen it, you wouldn't believe it. I didn't get the best view, driving northeast to Carefree. By the time I reached my destination, all that remained was a pencil-line of flame across the horizon and the beginning of the long deep indigo desert twilight. I hadn't intended to be there, but I had no place else to be. I had taken Lindsey to Sky Harbor that afternoon for her flight to Washington. Unlike me, she wasn't afraid of flying. So until I got the call that said she had reached the hotel in D.C., I would be at loose ends. From the airport, I went back to the courthouse. The phone was ringing when I unlocked the door.

"David. I need to see you. Can I see you tonight?"

I recognized Dana's voice without prompting.

"I don't keep office hours on Friday nights. Or don't you remember that from college?" She wasn't to blame for my mood, but hearing from her wasn't helping.

"David, please…" I could almost see her watery eyes tearing up.

"I'll be happy to give you the name and number of a detective who can handle this case," I said. "It's not good for my career for us to be seen together."

"But I have the proof you asked for. I have proof of the black-mail."

I just let dead air fill the phone. Somebody was pounding on the floor above, where the old jail was located before it was closed in the 1960s. I could claim a ghostly visitor and just hang up. "I have more for you. Maybe my information can help you find who really killed Louis Bell," she said.

"So tell me. I'm listening."

"I can't say this over the phone."

"So tell a detective."

"No." Her voice was lower, harder. "I need to see you, damn it. Don't you give a damn about that kid taking the fall for mur-dering Louis Bell? You know he didn't do it."

I stared at the ceiling, toward the old jail, then acquiesced. She gave me the name of a shop at El Pedregal, a fancy shopping center that's attached to the Boulders Resort. She didn't want anyone to recognize her, she said. I wasn't looking forward to the drive. I was dreading trying to explain to Peralta why I was making contact again with Dana Earley. But I was more than curious. If it hadn't been for Dana's lie, I would never have known Louis Bell. His murder would have been one more macabre Phoenix cop tale, even though it echoed close to home, in the similar killing of my neighbor, Alan Cordesman. With Dana, the coincidences became too much. She had launched me into something that was still playing out.

El Pedregal looks like a cross between an adobe Anasazi village and a Cold War blast shelter. But there was nothing to complain about with the natural surroundings: buttes made of gigantic boulders, each unique in its construction and the image it might concoct in the eye of an imaginative viewer. I had first seen all this before it was part of one of the priciest resorts in town, before the dry sun-bleached boulders were spectators on the edge of an emerald golf course. This night, there was not much to see beyond the black silhouettes of the buttes and the Carefree Mountains. The parking lot was mostly empty. As I walked toward the shops, most looked closed.

I checked the cell phone on my belt, wishing I would get Lindsey's call. I couldn't say that we had parted coolly that day. But neither had we gone beyond our brief spat of the day before, over my Patrick Blair comment. That night, I had made overtures with my fingers and mouth as we lay in bed. But she had kissed me and turned over. It wasn't a big deal. She hadn't refused. She had merely declined. A fine thing, words. Why was I reading anything into it? Was something more on her mind? Had I opened a line of a dangerous memory for her? Why did men never turn down sex? All important questions for which I had no answers.

I walked across the different plazas, pavilions, and ramadas. Here were the galleries and stores that made the tourists salivate: Canyon Lifestyles, the Blue Sage, the Desert Paradise Shop, Adelante. Every door was shut, although inside a few stores, a last employee was ending the day. A handful of resort guests strolled along, enjoying the low prices that the swanky hotels use in the hot weather. But low here was still out of my price range. A security guard gave me the once over and decided I was okay, for now. The temperature had dropped into the high nineties, but I was still sweating.

Finally, I came to the place Dana had mentioned, and it was open. *Milagro Glass Works* was etched on a large slab of glass outside the entrance. I stepped inside, said hello to a clerk sitting behind a counter, and looked for Dana. I was the only customer. I checked my watch and looked around. Several large Dale Chihuly blown-glass sculptures sat on display, with their colorful pipes and horns looking like the serpent-hair of Medusa. For those who didn't want to spend tens of thousands of dollars, several shelves held smaller items. There were flowers, shells, bowls, beads, and vases, in everything from the traditional to the wildly abstract. These were not exactly cheap, either. There was a lot of money in the world, and none of it going to honest cops. I was looking at a twisty sculpture called Rites of Summer when I saw something in my peripheral vision.

Some ancient reflex caused me to pull my head aside, and something heavy swooped past my ear. It still nicked me and a bubble of sharp pain burst along the right side of my head. I stepped back to see a tall, broad-shouldered man standing before me in a crouch. Taking up his right upper arm and shoulder was an elaborate, multicolored tattoo. He had a shaved head, a red bandanna over half his face, like in the Old West, and he held a long, black sap in his right hand. I hadn't seen one of those since my patrol days: a heavy piece of lead in a thick leather wrapping, attached to a strap that fit neatly in the hand. Some of the old cops had carried them.

"Asshole," he hissed, and lunged at me, swinging the sap at my head. I ducked and heard a crash that crossed several notes of the musical scale. One of the Chihulys disintegrated, sending orange, purple, and yellow shards like hard confetti into my face. I heard the clerk scream as I stumbled backward. He came again, faking punches with one hand while trying to get a good shot at me with the sap. My throat felt nearly closed off with panic, and I fought to get my wits back. Another fake punch and I grabbed his fist, trying to pull him down. Instantly my forearm exploded in agony as he brought the heavy weapon down on me. I let go.

Now there was about six feet between us, and I kept retreating toward the back of the store. He screamed in rage and tore down one of the shelves, scattering glass and display easels. I knew from academy days that the trick was to get close to the assailant, to step inside the reach of his arm so he couldn't swing, then do the takedown. I knew that. But for a few moments, I was nearly paralyzed with surprise and fear. My hand found a heavy slab of glass and I heaved it at his face. He ducked, but I used the moment of distraction. I willed my legs forward. Sure enough, when he realized what I was doing, it was too late. His hand came up holding the sap, but I was too close. With my left hand I grabbed his wrist, then brought my right arm behind his swinging arm. He pushed back but I was in a T-position, with my right foot planted securely behind me. I gave a rough push on his wrist, and the tension with my arm behind his elbow brought him down backward.

This is the point where the deputy quickly subdues the suspect, rolls him over, and cuffs him. But I was out of practice. We both crashed down to the hardwood floor, and somehow his knee ended up in my solar plexus. I rolled, so avoided the worst of it. But he scrambled out from under me, and by the time I got to my feet he was at the front door. I saw a flash of white and heard a groan. By the time I reached the threshold, I saw a guard on the concrete with a nasty gash in his head. Another guard was running my way. I flashed my badge and ordered him to call nine-one-one, then ran flat out after the tall man. I formed a description in my brain: six-four, shaved head, blue eyes, late twenties, wearing blue jeans and a white T-shirt, and carrying a red bandanna. The tattoo—I would need some time to remember details.

I lost him by the time I reached the parking lot. Suddenly I heard a guttural roar of a diesel engine and saw a jacked-up pickup round the corner. My assailant was at the wheel. I raced to Lindsey's Prelude. Its bumper sticker said, "Keep Honking, I'm Reloading." Inside was the Colt Python I had desperately needed moments before. I cranked it and sped toward Scottsdale Road. The truck was a black Dodge Ram, and the license plate was conveniently missing. Something was hanging below the rear bumper. It looked like a large set of testicles. He caught the green light at Carefree Highway, and I slammed through just as the amber was turning red. It was only then that I realized my cell phone had been knocked off in the melee. I only had a moment to worry about Lindsey in Washington. There was nothing to do but follow the truck.

It would have been nice if he had thought he was alone. But he was doing eighty and weaving in and out of traffic. He knew I was back there. To be sure, eighty miles an hour in Scottsdale on a Friday night was not much ahead of the flow of traffic. So much for my hope that he would attract the attention of Scottsdale PD. Still, the road was dark and treacherous. My ear and arm were really starting to hurt now, and my right hand was feeling a little numb. He just kept heading south. I knew what he wanted: the 101 beltway, which we would reach just before Bell Road. There, he could go anywhere he wanted.

He turned left at the 101 and really put on the power. I followed him and was doing nearly one hundred heading up the ramp. I had half a tank of gas and no plan other than to shoot him when he got where he was going. The freeway made its turn to the south and I was still on him. Traffic was thick as the highway went into the cut by Via Linda and curved, but he was quick and fearless. He threaded every needle, jumping into this lane, then the other, bullying any other vehicle out of his way. The oncoming lights blinded me at just the wrong time, and I lost his taillights. I had a sea of taillights, but I couldn't see the right ones. The description of a jacked-up diesel pickup truck in Phoenix, Arizona, was as bad as no description at all.

It was midnight when I got home. That made it three a.m. in Washington, D.C. The cops on the scene in Carefree thought it was an armed robbery gone wrong. I was certain it was something more. But Dana's phone went unanswered. At home, I made a martini and settled onto the leather sofa in the living room with William Taubman's biography of Nikita Khrushchev. Distract myself with Stalin's purges. It wasn't easy, because my heart was doing a tango inside my chest. I couldn't stop feeling every beat, and every beat felt wrong, felt fatal. I knew this was all an illusion. Some mistake of my brain chemistry. It didn't help that my ear felt as if it had been ripped off my head, even though the sap had inflicted only a small nick.

After half an hour, there was a knock on the door at the top of the book-lined stairway, and Robin let herself in. When she saw the shape I was in, she insisted on bringing me a Vicodin for the pain; she had been prescribed the drug for an injury while playing soccer. I took the pill and declined another martini. Robin poured herself a glass of red wine and we talked for what seemed like hours. I learned more about her past and told her a bit about mine. The easy talk evaporated my remaining suspicions about her. At some point, I fell into a heavy sleep, and when I woke up we were still on the sofa. She was asleep, her mane of straw-colored hair roiled up around her head. Her warm bare feet were in my lap, covered by my hands. I didn't recall how they got there.

# Chapter Twenty

Bobby Hamid's office overlooked Phoenix through a glass wall that must have been thirty feet long. His desk was a blond wood, chrome and glass aircraft-carrier deck, and its top was as uncluttered as the lid of a crypt. He was wearing a wheat-colored suit and a black T-shirt, wearing it like a male model, that is, if you didn't know that beyond his sleek looks sat something sinister. I didn't want to dwell on the office's other appointments, or how they had been funded, but I couldn't miss the beautiful Persian carpets under my feet, or the many pieces of Acoma pottery glistening in a large display case, lighted just right. It was hard to believe he'd started out as a student at Arizona State University, managing a strip club on the side.

"Ice picks and saps," he was saying, shaking his head and clucking in a strange feminine way. "Dr. Mapstone, you seem to have landed in some kind of 1940s noir movie."

"What do you know about it?"

"No, no!" he said sharply. "Dr. Mapstone, this is where you say something like, 'If it's a noir movie, I don't like how the story line is going.'"

I just looked at him and his view. The city was spoiled by the smog. Beyond the skyscrapers along Central Avenue, the South Mountains lurked in a brownish haze.

"You have no sense of play, David," he said. "I can understand, with Miss Lindsey being gone…"

The worry point directly below my breastbone started sending out red alerts. I said, "It really disturbs me that you know that."

"I also know what it means to be the 'odd man out,' as the expression goes." He leaned back and put his manicured hands behind his head. "The intellectual in a city of developers and construction workers..." I let him run on, his sentences a smart parade of empty words. It was part of his act. My head still hurt from my sap-on-ear encounter of Friday night; that, and the combination of two martinis and Robin's painkiller. I had left her sleeping on the sofa, and quietly went into the bedroom for another couple of hours' sleep. Lindsey called at six a.m., before her meeting with the feds, and her voice did a lot to heal me. But I didn't tell her how afraid I had been when the tall man came at me. I sanitized the incident. I knew she wouldn't want that, but there was nothing she could do from Washington except worry. I had worried all weekend with nothing to show for it. Now it was Monday, and I could look forward to a week of worry. I tuned back in to Bobby again: "...a historian in an age where people care nothing for history. A man who dresses well, when many men wear their clothes like adolescents. You know, they spend all their money on electronics instead. I'm not that way, of course. I think that's why we appreciate each other. History, ideas, a sense of style, beautiful women..."

"We appreciate each other until the sheriff puts you away for several lifetimes. But I do value your expertise. That's why I'm here."

"Ah, I am your, quote, organized crime expert, unquote," he said merrily. "Very well. Both weapons are quaint. Consider the three teenagers executed last night behind the 202 Freeway wall. I know this from the newspaper, by the way. But they were shot, pop, pop, pop." He did it with his index finger, aiming toward the far wall. Even so, it stirred a kind of unease in me. Bobby went on, "This is efficiency in the post-modern capitalist style. You have a non-performing asset, you get it off the books as quickly and neatly as possible." He studied his cuticle. "The only reason someone would use an ice pick or a sap is to make a point."

"Which is?"

"How would I know this, Dr. Mapstone? You are the History Shamus, as Miss Lindsey calls you. May I fix you a drink? There are some amazing red wines out of Australia now, you know."

"I don't care," I said. "Somebody tried to smash me up along with the Chihuly sculptures, and I don't think it was for writing a book. That leaves me with the other issue that's taken my time lately. Why would someone use an ice pick to murder a guy who owns some check-cashing outlets, and then do it again with some old guy who owns nothing but some worthless land?"

"Were there fingerprints on the ice picks?" Bobby asked in the voice of a surgeon at a medical conference.

"No, that's another thing that bothers me," I said.

"But I thought they had charged that unfortunate, disadvantaged Hispanic youth with that crime."

"Well, what if he didn't do it?"

"Ah, a who-done-it." He said each word carefully. "Maybe it's one of those serial killers that seem drawn to our fine city. Maybe the two victims shared some hidden connection."

"I'm not after Sherlock Holmes, Bobby," I said sharply. "You know things and hear things. Hell, you do things."

"Oh, David, please. Sheriff Peralta fills you with fantasies and half-truths. Look out that window. That's where the money is made. In real estate, building, retailing, and tourism. Why would I need to break the law?"

"I thought you were a venture capitalist. Now you're a developer? Better find a story and stick to it."

"Alas, the Phoenix economy is not what the chamber of commerce types claim," he said. "All my VC investments are in California and Austin. Phoenix is not exactly on the cutting edge. So as a businessman here, of course I invest in real estate. Everybody does. It's the only economy we have. Someday the bubble will burst, of course. Then I will move into Treasuries."

I gave an exaggerated yawn, even though my forearm hurt like hell when I raised it. Nasty things, saps.

Bobby said, "I've heard the Samoans from LA are trying to move in on the meth trade here. Think of it as a maturing industry with many scattered players that is attracting takeover artists. But they don't seem like the ice pick types to me. The check-cashing outlets? Some are compromised with the smuggling trade, which is an international, well-capitalized operation. That might be a more profitable avenue for you."

"How so?"

He shrugged. "My suspicions as a civilian would probably be useless to you, History Shamus. It does strain my credulity to believe this young man, Esparza, walked into a crowded casino and killed the man for his wallet. What was his name? Bell?" He leaned toward me. "How is your book coming?"

"It's coming," I said.

"I wonder if I'll be in it?" he chirped. "I wonder if Miss Gretchen will be there? She certainly had edge, as they say."

I tried to ignore him. "What do you know about Tom Earley?" I asked.

His thin lips stretched into an icy smile. "A slick character, I think," Bobby said.

I just waited, watching jets in the distance land at Sky Harbor. Only four days until Lindsey came home.

Finally, Bobby said, "Mr. Earley is deep into our two growth industries: real estate and conservative politics. All I know is what I read in the papers, as Walter Winchell said."

"Will Rogers," I corrected. "Ever met Earley?"

"Once, at a fundraiser for Barrow Neurological Institute. It was at the Phoenician, as I recall. He had his wife with him. A pretty woman with red hair. Do you know them? Are they connected with your murders?"

"Thanks for your help, Bobby," I said, rising to leave. "If you hear anything…"

He nodded, and rose to shake my hand.

"David," he said, "you have a tendency to over-think things. Sometimes there's not an elaborate plot or cosmic evil at work. Sometimes it's just simple, feral greed."

My feet had crossed a hundred thousand dollars in Persian rugs when his voice came again. "Why were you at El Pedregal? You don't strike me as the resort type."

I turned to face him. "I was meeting someone."

"Ah," he said. I left it at that.

# Chapter Twenty-One

For a place in the desert, my town sure had a lot of deep ends. One day, I was just another guy with a Ph.D. and a badge writing a book. The next, I was defying the sheriff's direct orders, going to meet my mystery soccer mom, who happened to be married to a powerful politician who would like nothing better than to see me pulling espresso shots at Starbucks. Only she doesn't show up, and I was the china shop for a bull with a taste for old-time gangland hardware. I was in over my head. Why stop there, Mapstone? Keep going. If you really work hard, you can be unemployed by the time Lindsey gets back from Washington.

That knowledge hadn't kept me from making two trips to Gilbert over the weekend. The house looked deserted. I didn't even hear from the Rottweilers. Finally, I went next door, where a smooth-faced man yielded to my badge-based way of making friends and influencing people. He told me the Earleys had left for Europe on vacation. Was anything wrong?, he asked. *More than you know.* Was there any way he could help?, he asked. *No, and I'm sorry to disappoint the neighborhood gossips. Just think of me as collecting for the sheriff's DARE program. Or think nothing at all.* I was thinking too much, as Bobby noted. Dana lured me into a trap. That's what my gut said. Or had the blackmailer been real, and somehow either scared her off or…? She had definitely left for the airport Saturday morning, the morning after the episode in the glass shop. The neighbor had seen her with her husband and children, getting in the SUV.

I spent the rest of Monday in my courthouse garret. Yet somehow the pages I had written seemed stale. Duke Ellington through the headphones failed to comfort me. The archives that I had carefully laid out on the big counsel's table looked at me with disinterest. I wrote two pages over and over on the Macintosh; the process lacked even the bathos of filling wastebaskets with wadded-up paper sheets, as I had in grad school. Eventually, I closed up shop, grabbed a burrito at Ramiro's, and went home. The only thing to show for the day was Lindsey's goodnight call.

The next day, I rode the bus downtown, checked out an unmarked Crown Vic and took a road trip. It wasn't the kind of trip most people took willingly. I stopped at a Circle K to buy several bottles of water and put them on ice in a small ice chest. I was going to a place that was about as close to Yuma County as you could get and still be under the jurisdiction of Mike Peralta, and I was doing it on the first day of summer. It couldn't even be reached directly. So I took Interstate 10 south to Casa Grande and headed west on I-8. Seemingly everywhere but the Indian reservation there was new framing for subdivisions. Where were these people going to work? All building, selling, furnishing, servicing, and financing new housing, I supposed. Where was the water going to come from? This part of the state was using more groundwater than was being replenished. Nobody seemed to want to talk about that one. Most of the newcomers didn't even know where their water came from—in their civilized minds, the answer was the water tap, of course! On I-8, the subdivisions fell behind, replaced by cotton fields, then empty desert. Follow the interstate far enough and you ended up in San Diego. I had lived a very different life there long ago. I didn't think of it often now. I missed the pleasant weather.

At a nothing exit called Sentinel, I left our equivalent of the Roman roads and turned toward wilderness, where barbarians were, perhaps, included. The road quickly turned to dirt and gravel, rising and falling gradually with the land. Scrubby desert surrounded me, with strange mountain shapes off in the distance north and south. After a while, I came to the little hamlet of Hyder. When the mainline of the Southern Pacific Railroad was built to Phoenix eighty years before, Hyder was one more place to put a water tower, to keep the locomotives from expiring like dehydrated horses in the blazing wilderness. In more recent years, you heard stories about the desert rats, hermits, and one-time hippies out here. Back in the early '90s, the Sunset Limited passenger train had derailed nearby—sabotage, and unsolved. The village was its own little world of forlorn trailers and folks who wanted to be left alone. This day, it looked deserted in the manner of desert towns when the temperature is over one hundred. I took a dirt road back to the east, following the old railroad. After a few miles, I found the place where the Bell brothers had lived out their last years.

It was a small trailer in a clearing between the road and the railroad, sheltered from the wind by raggedy tamarisk trees. The metal walls looked faded and ready to fall off, but the roof held a new-looking satellite dish. The entrance was guarded by a heavy security door with yellow paint peeling in potato-chip sized patches. I parked as a dust devil cut across the rail embankment and battered the car briefly before heading south. That gave me time to get the keys to the place out of an evidence envelope. As I stepped out, the heat hit me like opening the door to an oven set on high. I looked around. There was a bedraggled school bus, maybe two hundred yards down the road. Otherwise I was alone. No cars. No sound. Getting inside the trailer meant climbing a rickety wooden stairway. Underneath were years of old cans—coffee, chili, tuna, and God knows what else. I tried not to imagine the rattlesnake, Gila monster, black widow, and scorpion refuge they had created.

The lightweight inner door came open with a shove, and a hot, stale smell hit me. Old food, tobacco smoke, gym socks— something like that. The inside of the trailer went with the odor. It was impossible to tell if someone had ransacked the place or if the brothers had lived this way. Old clothes, tools, newspapers, pieces of cardboard, and beer cans were everywhere. There was too much furniture for the limited space, and all of it junk from other eras, right down to the beanbag chair that had been patched with duct tape. In one corner stood a giant plasma-screen TV, wildly out of place. A window air conditioning unit miraculously worked. I tried to be as methodical as possible. There had been no crime committed here, so the deputies had made only a cursory search. They might have come back, but they had a suspect. Their inventory of items retrieved from the Bell trailer was small and of no help to me.

I moved slowly through the confined spaces, checking my blind spots, coughing from the dust that inevitably seeped in. Even though the air conditioning worked, I couldn't get the lights on. If not for the sunlight breaking through the ancient curtains, the inside would have been even murkier. I kept checking those curtains, to see what was outside, who was coming down the road. There was only one door in and out. When the wind hit the walls and made the old sheet-metal rattle, my hands started shaking. Calm down, Mapstone.

One thing about country living was simplicity. Atop the peeling linoleum counter was what passed as the brothers' desk. But there were no bills for credit cards, cell phones, or water softener. Just a stack of girlie magazines, some old lottery tickets, and a letter from the county. Inside was a second notice demanding back taxes. I slipped it in my pocket, wondering if the parcel was the one where Harry Bell was laid to rest. Death and taxes, indeed.

The drawers and closets were similarly unhelpful. Old men's clothes and underwear. Under a pile of work shirts, I found a .38 revolver that looked like it hadn't been cleaned or fired in decades. No property records. No indication of an involvement with the Earleys. No photographs. No blackmailer kit. Behind some muddy shoes I found an old frame, the kind bought for a dollar in the kind of stores that were once called five and dime stores. Inside was a faded certificate, the honorable discharge from the Army of Harry Truman Bell, dated 1968. Bobby Kennedy and Martin Luther King had been assassinated. The cities were in flames. The Vietnam War was going badly. I was at Kenilworth School. Lindsey was born.

What is the sum of a life? What will the cops find if misfortune comes calling? Lindsey and I have a house full of the personal and peculiar. They would find her Oaxacan carvings and Day of the Dead art; her hardback collection of Russian literature and everything written by and about J.R.R. Tolkien. There would be my collection of suits that were usually too hot to wear in Phoenix, too many ties, a bag full of old presidential campaign buttons that was probably worth something, files of my old publications in history journals and background material for the two obscure history books I wrote. Books and books and books. And photographs by the boxful, from one showing Grandmother and Grandfather on their wedding day to another, taken nine decades later, of Lindsey and me on our day. Life is stuff. Most of Robin's things were in a storage unit on Thomas Road; I had lived that way once. Peralta and Sharon had yet to fully divide their household, the accumulations of thirty years of marriage. Yet here in this dusty trailer, I was most struck by the absence of much that was personal. When I stepped through the outside door half an hour later, I still didn't know the Bell brothers. I didn't know if they were blackmailers or victims or nobodies.

Someone was waiting for me.

# Chapter Twenty-Two

"Whatcha doin?" he called, in a friendly enough voice.

I showed my star to a man in a wheelchair. He was parked in the dirt maybe ten feet from the bottom of the steps.

"I live over there," he said, indicating the school bus. He couldn't have been more than twenty. He had a small face the color of the desert dirt, with hundreds of brown freckles. It was a face marked off by long brown hair, parted in the middle, and it carried a pleasant expression. Those were sometimes the ones who killed you as they smiled. But his frame was tiny, barely taking up half of the wheelchair, and I was happy to see his hands were free of firearms.

"Terrible thing what happened to Louie," he said. "And on top of Harry dying last winter..."

I asked him if he wanted to get out of the sun and talk. He said he liked the sun. I slipped on my sunglasses and started sweating. Leaning up against the car wasn't such a good idea, either.

"I live over there," he said again. "It's cheap. Got this way 'cause I fell off a roof. I used to do construction, up in Phoenix. One time, I thought I might like to be a deputy, like you. Help people. But I fell and can't work anymore. The contractor wouldn't pay workman's comp."

"I don't think that's legal," I ventured.

"He's my dad," he said, "the contractor. We was working on some houses out in Surprise. He said I wasn't legally on his payroll. It was just me and the illegals, the Mexicans, working for him, and none of us was covered. Course, I never thought I'd get hurt. Nineteen and you feel immortal. It's okay out here. I like the quiet. Train doesn't even come by much anymore. Every now and then the illegals come through on foot, heading north to the city. I just let 'em be. Sometimes, if the wind's right, you can hear the bombing down on the gunnery range. Louie and Harry was good neighbors. It's lonelier without them."

I opened the car and pulled out two bottles of water, giving him one. Then I wheeled him into the shade of the tamarisks. He didn't protest. From behind, I could see his hair pulled back in a ponytail and braided like a kite's tail. On his forearm was a tattoo of an eagle—was I the last person in America without body art? He said his name was Davey Crockett. He spelled it. I asked him to tell me what Harry and Louie were like.

"Didn't know Harry real well. He was pretty sick the whole time I was out here. So I'd come over and check on him. He could get out here in front, and we'd just sit and watch the world go by, which isn't much out here. But it's peaceful, you know? Harry'd been married once, and he'd talk to his ex-wife occasionally on the phone. Then he'd go off on the worst cussing jag…"

"Ever meet the ex?"

"Nope. She never came out here, far as I can tell. Harry was a hard one to get close to. Full of piss and vinegar, as my mom would say. He hated the government, sure they were going to come get him."

"What for?"

"Beats me," Davey Crockett said. "He listened to talk radio for hours. He'd smoke and drink and listen to his radio. Louie, now he was more personable. He was a good guy—helped me get groceries and stuff when my mom and sister couldn't make it out here. He loaded me up in his pickup a few times and took me to the casinos. It was nice to get around people for a while."

I asked him where the brothers got their money.

"Social security, I guess," he said. "They didn't have much, as far as I could tell. I think each one only had two or three pairs of pants. See I notice things. I might have made a good deputy."

"I bet you probably would have been. You knew the brothers how long?"

"I've been out here for three years this July."

"And they didn't seem like they had much money. How about cars? What did they drive?"

"Just an old Chevy pickup, 1978, Scottsdale trim package," he said knowledgeably.

"That's it? Not two cars?"

"No, Harry was too sick to drive. When he died, a doc came out and signed the death certificate and Louie and some of the guys from Hyder loaded him in the truck to bury him out in the desert. Harry was really firm about that. He didn't want to be embalmed. He was convinced it was some kind of government conspiracy, where your organs were sold off to aliens. Sounded kinda weird to me. But that was Harry…"

"What about Louie? Was he paranoid?"

"Nope, not a bit of it. We'd sit out and drink at night, watch the stars, talk about life and women. Louie'd never been married, but he'd had his share when he was a younger dude."

I asked, "Anybody who would want to hurt Louie?"

The man shook his small head. "Nobody I can think of. It's pretty isolated out here, as you can tell. But, I'll tell you, I've probably seen more comings and goings at this trailer since Louie was killed, than in three years' time."

"Comings and goings?"

"There's you." He counted off on slender fingers. "There was a couple of cop cars with deputies. They told me what happened to Louie, and they spent some time looking around. Then, maybe a couple of days later, I woke up around midnight to take my pain pills and there was a truck, kinda parked right over by Louie's trailer. Stayed there for at least an hour, and he kept the headlights on, trained at the trailer. I saw a man come out, and he got into the truck and it drove off."

"Pickup truck?"

He nodded. "And then, maybe a week later, I saw the same truck. He came after midnight, and shut off his lights and went inside again. This time he stayed longer. I don't know how long, 'cause I fell asleep."

"What kind of truck? Could you see?"

"It was dark," he said. Then he brightened. "But it was a Dodge Ram pickup, extended cab, diesel. It was black, with chrome accessories. And…"

"And?"

"Had a set of balls dangling from the rear bumper, that kinda amused me."

I took in a sharp breath, and said, "You could see all that?"

He made a face. "It'd been there before, a couple times before Louie was killed. In the daytime. Dude would knock on the door and go in, and they'd talk a while, then he'd leave. Louie was always upset afterwards. Really nervous. But he wouldn't talk to me about it."

"What did this guy in the truck look like?"

Davey closed his eyes tightly. He said, "White guy, probably thirty years old, shaved head." He opened his eyes. "He had this really big tat, you know? On his right shoulder and arm. He wore a tank top every time, to show it off. Kinda scary looking, you ask me. He didn't know I was watching. But I told you, I notice things."

All that was missing from the description was a bandanna and a sap—this was my adversary from the other night. I asked, "Any chance you noticed a license tag?"

"Nope. Never thought I'd need to. Want me to get it if he comes back again?"

"No, Davey," I said. "Don't let him see you. But if he does show up again, give me a call." I handed him a business card, asked if there was anything I could do for him, and when the answer was no, headed back to the city.

# Chapter Twenty-Three

It was a little after five p.m. on Friday when there was a tap on the pebbled glass of my office door. I invited the knocker in, and it was Robin. She was wearing a calf-length skirt with a blue paisley pattern and a white knit top. It was the most feminine I had seen her dress, but the change didn't end there. She was wearing makeup. The transformation was remarkable. I won't say it made her beautiful, but she looked very attractive, and I told her so.

"Thank you," she said, and sat down facing me. "I'm under orders from Lindsey to take both us out—me because I'm mending from a broken heart, although I never had my heart that involved with Edward. And you, because Lindsey told me the bad news."

It was true. Lindsey would be in Washington for another two weeks. The computer security breach had become big news, affected dozens of companies, and another penetration had happened the night before. She had been assigned to a task force, and she couldn't tell me much more. They would also be monitoring her phone calls, and I wouldn't even be able to come up and visit her—she would be working every day and night. If the feds had been listening, they would know our call hadn't gone well. Her delay would mean we couldn't leave on our long-anticipated vacation. I knew she was as disappointed as me, maybe more so. But I had been looking forward to time away from Phoenix, away from the heat and the endless lookalike subdivisions and crackpot politicians and their wives. I had been short with Lindsey, and after we hung up I was instantly remorseful.

"You're really dependent on her, aren't you?" Robin asked, looking at me with an intense expression, as if trying to read my thoughts.

"I think it's mutual," I said. "I hope so. What are you in the mood for?"

I took her for drinks to Tom's Tavern, where Peralta joined us after making the rounds with some politicians at other tables. They seemed pleased to see each other. The conversation was light, and, as usual, Robin could talk a lot. But she talked about interesting things, in this case eight months she had spent in Paris, and I was content to listen. Then Peralta left to give a speech. Robin vetoed my suggestion that we go to the galleries over on Roosevelt Row—"I go there all the time"—although I think the real reason was she thought it was too young a crowd for me. So, after being told the wait for a table at Pizzeria Bianco was four hours, we went to dinner at Lombardi's at Arizona Center and then saw a movie. A few days later, I couldn't have told you the title. Afterward, Robin wanted a nightcap, so we swung by Portland's.

I noticed she had drunk bourbon when Peralta was around, but maybe the two were not connected. At Portland's, she drank red wine, and I ordered a snifter of cognac. She held her liquor and was full of stories and opinions. But she also seemed genuinely interested when I talked about history and culture. I found myself liking her and setting aside my earlier misgivings.

She asked, "So how's your case going, David?"

"Well, it's not really my case. Peralta doesn't want me nosing around it."

"Oh, he seemed nice enough when we saw him."

I said, "That's because you were around." Her lips made a small secret smile, and I talked about "my" case. It did feel that way to me, and it had since Dana deposited her bogus letter on my desk months before. Since my trip to the Bell trailer, I had called the doctor who signed the death certificate. He had said Harry Bell suffered from emphysema, a bad heart, high blood pressure, and bleeding ulcers. Harry wouldn't take medicine or take care of himself. To the doc, the death had all the signs of a stroke. Then I had read the case file on Louie Bell's accused killer, Jesus Esparza. Even the county attorney agreed the man had the mind of an eight-year-old. His rap sheet had no indication of violence. His prints were not found on the ice pick. Together, the evidence didn't conjure the image of a killer who could dispatch someone in a crowded casino with an ice pick, and never even knock the victim's body off its stool before the slot machine. I believed what the kid's public defender said: he picked up the wallet from the floor, and never knew Bell was dead.

"So it sounds like they got the wrong guy," Robin said, patting my hand. "You rock, David."

"That isn't the way the sheriff sees it," I said. Not only that, but I still hadn't heard from Dana Earley. Not so much as a "Sorry we missed each other that night in Carefree. Hope you didn't get a concussion."

"You and the sheriff act like brothers, do you know that?"

"No," I said. I would think about that one later. I went on, "Maybe I can talk to Patrick Blair about the case. He was the detective who investigated it."

"Yes, the pretty one," Robin said. "He has an eye for Lindsey. I bet it really sucks that he's in Washington right now, too, for that police convention. Lindsey told me he was going to be there, and she was looking forward…"

She saw my face and put a hand on my shoulder. "Oh, David. I'm sorry. Shit. I thought she would have told you."

"Whatever," I said, and ordered another cognac. I encouraged Robin to tell me more about her time in Paris, and she talked. It was shaping up to be a really bad day. I guess I had given my wife reason to censor herself. But had I? It's not as if I flew into a rage at the mention of the man's name. I had occasionally lampooned him, although the last time I had done that it brought Lindsey's rebuke. I had never been given a reason to mistrust Lindsey. Why hadn't she simply told me about Blair? Robin, meanwhile, segued into talking about her lovers. She said Edward had never been a serious relationship. Her most passionate lover had been a polo player from Argentina; they had continued to see each other intermittently after he had married an heiress in Charleston. "I couldn't compete on the money front," she said. I half listened.

"I'm kind of surprised you and Lindsey ended up together," she said. That brought me out of my reverie. Robin looked at me with an expression I can only describe as kindly. She went on, "I mean, Lindsey always liked the bad-boy type."

"Maybe I'm a bad boy," I said gamely. She raised an eyebrow and toasted me. I clinked her glass with my snifter, and watched the light play off the dark amber hue of the liquor. The conversation made me feel uncomfortable and vulnerable. A man of the world shouldn't feel that way, should he?

"Anyway," I said, "however it happened, it's the best thing that ever happened to me."

We were both at least a little tipsy when we left. She put her hand through my arm and I let her. I couldn't drink the volume I once could. We drove the short distance to Cypress Street, where most of the houses had turned in for the night. Inside the door, I thanked her for her company.

"I'm sorry if I brought you down, David."

"You didn't."

"I think she made a good choice," Robin said. "A good catch. Even if you will be her first husband."

She said it without smiling. I just looked at her.

"Even if you two stay together, men die early. And she's several years younger. It's just the actuarial tables."

"OK," I said. "On that cheery note, we'll say goodnight." I could hear the harshness in my voice.

Robin cocked her head and put a hand on her hip. For a long moment, she looked at me. She said, "You know, David, I can't decide if you're threatened by me, or if you're attracted to me and don't know what to do about it."

She instantly had me against the wall and was kissing me, her tongue warm and agile inside my mouth, her body connecting on all points. I took her shoulders and held her back.

"Robin! Are you crazy? This can't happen."

She evaded my hands and was against me again. Her mouth applied gentle suction as she kissed. She said, "That's not what your body is saying, I can feel it." She held my head in her hands, and she was very strong.

I managed to turn my head aside.

I said, "Robin, I'm sorry if you got the wrong message from me. I'm not interested."

"I got the right message," she said. She was rubbing my groin, which wasn't supporting the decision I was trying to make. She said, "We'll have some fun, and then it will be over. If you want it to be. I don't want to be married and settled down like big sister, if she wants to be." I grabbed her hand, and she pinned me again, kissing me deeply.

This time I pushed her away with some force. Her eyes bored into me.

She said, "Let it happen, David. You want it more than anything right now. You don't even know where Lindsey is. You don't even know if she's alone. We could have a mutual grudge fuck, me against Edward and you…"

"No."

She added, a playful lilt to her voice, "I won't tell. I won't stain your precious honor."

"I won't hurt Lindsey," I said. An interior voice said, *You overestimate my honor. There was a time when I would have already had you down on the floor.* I moved sideways and away from the wall.

"Every man wants to do sisters," she said, following me with a buccaneer's smile on her face. "I did a pair of brothers once. It was fun as hell. Later you can tell me how I'm different from her, and how we're the same."

She advanced on me again, and I started to push her away. She batted away one arm, then the other, and pinned me against the edge of the bookshelves. "You're too slow, David. I took kickboxing for four years," she laughed. "Maybe I'll just rape reluctant David. Give him the ultimate excuse." She pressed her breasts against me and ran her hands over me. "Not all of you is reluctant."

"We're both drunk," I said, pushing against her. "I won't hurt Lindsey, and I know you wouldn't want that, either. She really loves you…"

Robin kissed me, her tongue burrowing past my teeth, and she started unbuttoning my shirt. When I moved my head, she whispered in my ear, "David is reasoning with Robin. David is trying to give himself lots of excuses for when this finally happens, when it happens and he really loves it, that he did everything he could to stop it."

"It's not going to happen," I said. "You're drunk. Lindsey would be ashamed of both of us."

"You don't know Lindsey as well as you think you do," Robin whispered, her breath hot on my neck. "I bet you don't know she has a kid."

The edge of the tall bookshelves was digging into my back. I said, "Lindsey doesn't want to have children."

"Well it's too late for that," she whispered insistently. "When she was 16, she had a baby."

"That's not true. She never told me that."

"She wouldn't tell you. She had a boy. She didn't want to give him up for adoption, but Linda made her. Then Linda made her join the Air Force, to get away from Ryan. That was the father. Now he was a bad boy. Nice try, Linda, but the barn door was already open, don't ya know. Lindsey had a real thing for him, a real addiction. They got back together a few years later. She found him. They lived together until he killed himself on his motorcycle. But I know Lindsey still wants to find that baby she had with Ryan. I know it. I know the truth hurts, David. I know you want to be Lindsey's true love. It just didn't work out that way. Let Robin make things better…"

I was dully aware that Robin was holding me like a drunken dance partner. When I felt her kiss me again, I shoved her away. She shrugged and smiled and mounted the stairs that led to the garage apartment. She said, "I'll leave the door unlocked for you, baby."

# Chapter Twenty-Four

It's wisdom as common as a child's saying: two's company and three's a crowd. My personal paradise with Lindsey had become badly crowded by Robin. It was enough overpopulation to make old Malthus turn over in his grave. I'd been mind-fucked by some pros—but Robin was setting a new standard. If she had her way, the congress wouldn't have stopped with my mind. I knew Lindsey could sense something wrong in my voice from 2,000 miles away. As we talked, I could hear a beep every few seconds—her federal minder—sounding like a supervisor monitoring a sales call. We couldn't talk about anything real. Was she really working all the time in a highly secure environment? Or was there time off to see Patrick Blair? Could what Robin told me possibly be true? "I'll be back soon, Dave," she said, "so don't fall in love with my sister." And she laughed her fine, crystal laugh. For just a second, I thought about telling her that Robin had made a pass at me. But then I would want to say more, ask more.

I spent the weekend with my Khrushchev biography, mostly sitting in the study, sometimes with Lester Young and Sinatra on my headphones. How the world had changed—I found myself feeling a little sorry for the Soviet leader. Of course that was hindsight sweetened by the way the Cold War had ended. When K was in power and I was a child, I had lived in mortal fear of nuclear war. There were missile silos around Tucson back then. Reflecting on all that from the safety of my leather chair made the mortal information given me by Robin seem small in comparison.

If I were drafting a biography, I would write, "Mapstone's family situation became complicated that summer." I tried to sift this new information at a cool remove: that Patrick Blair was also in Washington with Lindsey; and that Lindsey had a baby, and now would be the mother of a grown man. It might have no more truth than any number of myths that historians are paid to debunk. But I had about the same cool distance as the SUVs tailgating on Central that Monday as I rode the bus downtown. On the sidewalk, a man wearing nothing but dirty cargo shorts walked north with a hand-lettered cardboard sign. It said, "Jesus is Coming." The weekend had been all anti-climax. I saw Robin as she was coming and going, and both of us acted as if nothing had happened. But the house seemed to lack oxygen, and I was happy to go back to work. I stopped for a mocha at the Starbucks on Adams Street, then walked in the shade of the buildings over to the courthouse. Somehow I wasn't sweating yet—it was only in the high nineties. So I took the winding steps up to the fourth floor.

Even though the county was chronically short on office space, my end of the building was deserted. It involved some ancient dispute between this and that department over the offices, with neither winning. It was a shame because the renovation had restored the 1929 beauty to the place, with dark wooden doors and transoms, pebbled glass, and dignified light globes. Many days the custodians don't even turn on the hall lights and today was no exception. That's why the light at the end of the corridor made me slow my pace. My door was standing open. It was probably a lazy cleaning crew. But given my luck lately, I pulled out the Python. My footsteps suddenly sounded horrendously loud. Another five steps and I came in the door with the revolver in one hand and a Starbucks cup in the other. I swept the room until the barrel rested on the compact form of Kate Vare.

"You look ridiculous," she said. "Put that away. They shouldn't even let you be armed. You could be like Barney Fife, and Peralta could keep one bullet for you in his pocket."

I tended to like cops, but in Vare's case it was easy to make an exception. As Phoenix PD's top cold-case expert, she was convinced I was always on her turf. It didn't help that she had the personality of my vinegar-faced fourth-grade teacher, who, come to think of it, she rather dressed like today. She wore a dark plaid skirt and high-necked blouse. Unlike Mrs. Mulcahey of the fourth grade, Kate had ash blond hair in a Martha Stewart style, and carried a 9-mm Glock on her hip. She sat on my desk, absently twirling her black pump on her right toe.

"Why are you here?" I demanded. "Why don't you ever knock? Did you just break in?"

"Somebody did," she said.

I turned back to the door. The lock had been completely removed, as if some tunneling device had bored right through it. I noticed it lying in pieces on the wood floor.

"Very professional job, too," she said.

I looked around, and the office looked much like I had left it on Friday. If someone had been inside, he had been very careful, or been interrupted before he could ransack it.

"What are you working on?" Vare asked coyly.

"What business is it of yours?" I walked around, inspecting shelves, opening file drawers, feeling the vague shock and violation of the burglarized.

"You are such a bastard, Mapstone," she said. Her bony lower jaw worked silently. "I know you were down at headquarters last week."

"I'm compiling a manuscript," I said grudgingly. "About the historic cases. Peralta wants it."

She laughed loudly, a surprisingly humorless sound coming from Kate. "You are such a bad liar, Mapstone. You were looking at the Alan Cordesman homicide file."

I could feel my face flushing. David Mapstone, master of deceit. Wait until Lindsey asked me if I kissed her sister or let her massage my crotch. Yes, while I was at the PD working on the book, I had stopped by Homicide and asked to see the file.

"Why do you care?" I said, finally sitting at my desk. I sipped the mocha, which was starting to go room temperature.

"Prove to me that I shouldn't," she said. "For all I know, Cordesman ties back to a cold case, and you're doing one of your famous end-runs. All the glory to Mapstone and the Sheriff's Office."

"I've never…"

"What the hell are you holding out?" she demanded. "I swear to God I'll complain to Chief Wilson, get a court order, arrest your ass right this second!"

Now it was her turn to flush. I thought she was going to have a stroke right there on the desktop.

"Kate, you really need to relax. I don't have anything. The guy was killed a block away from my house. I was curious."

"You discovered the body," she said.

"I was called by a neighbor who discov…"

"You should have been arrested as a material witness. That's what I would have done."

I said, "You really have this thing about handcuffs…"

"You know something," she went on. "I don't know what the hell it is. I went through the computer, checked all my red-flag files. I can't find anything that involves an ice pick through the ear. But I obviously missed something."

"You didn't," I said. "There's no historic case involved."

"Yeah, well, then without that there's no case for the state," she said, leaning forward, her small hands on her lap. She went on, "The county attorney's not going to prosecute this. There's no physical evidence linking Esparza to the Cordesman crime scene, like there is with Louis Bell. Not one hair. Not one fiber. Not one print."

"Well, I didn't think Esparza did either one."

"You bastard," she said quietly, standing. "I knew you were holding out."

"I'm not!" I nearly shouted. "Esparza has the mind of an eight-year-old, and this is a smart crime. Sure, they caught the kid with the wallet. But none of the rest of it adds up. And why would the kid kill these two very different victims in such different places?" I didn't mention Dana or the fake letter that led me to the dead brother in the desert.

"Esparza is a burglar," she said.

"That just makes my point. Cordesman wasn't missing anything."

Her eyes narrowed. "Not true, Mapstone. Burglary got a call from an insurance company on Friday. Their initial inventory of his possessions had been wrong. Cordesman owned a diamond ring. It belonged to his great-grandmother, and it was insured for twenty-five thousand dollars. It's missing."

"That's it? From what I could see, he had some expensive electronics, a computer, stuff you could fence easily. Why leave all that and take the ring?"

"You tell me, Barney Fife."

I felt my stomach aching that Kate Vare ache. I said, "Maybe he lost it. Maybe he pawned it."

"Maybe," she said. "I called Cordesman's brother in Reno. He's the beneficiary. Apparently Alan had a new girlfriend. But he didn't tell his brother her name or anything about her. Maybe he gave it to the girlfriend. Or maybe she took it after she shoved the ice pick in his brain."

I sipped the mocha and said nothing. Two's company and three's a crowd. Louis Bell and Alan Cordesman murdered in the same manner. And then there was Harry Bell, apparently dead from natural causes. But he was the bait used by Dana to draw me into…what? Something important enough to make somebody toss my office.

"Earth to Mapstone!" Vare said. She was standing before me, hands on her hips. "This is not a one-way street, Barney Fife."

"True, Thelma Lou," I said. She squinted and turned her small mouth down. I doubted her Mayberry knowledge was that complete. "Fair is fair, but so far there's nothing about this case that should interest either of us…"

"Give it up, or I swear to God…"

"The only thing Louie Bell owned in the world besides a trailer by the railroad tracks was one thousand acres of land. He inherited it when his older brother died. It's way the hell west of Tonopah, so it's not worth that much. But the county has tax liens against it. He was way behind in paying his taxes."

"How do you know this?"

"There was a notice from the county at his trailer. I took it when I was down there last week." She started to speak, but I talked over her. "I talked to a neighbor kid. He told me some guy kept coming by and harassing Bell. I don't know about what. The same guy came back, after Louie Bell was killed, and went through the trailer."

"Did he have a description?" she demanded.

"Not much," I said. I told her about the Dodge pickup and the man with the shaved head and tattooed shoulder. I didn't tell her that he had tried to rearrange my brains in the glass gallery. We were even in the information swap.

She stared at me warily, slowly shaking her head.

"I just don't trust you," she said. "And even if I did, it wouldn't get me anywhere. The casino case belongs to the feds. Dealing with them is even worse than dealing with you."

# Chapter Twenty-Five

The city kept growing. Slogans and euphemisms played as big a role as "Go West Young Man" did in the nineteenth century. Now it was selling a dream "set within a stunning landscape...As rare as the splendor of the Sonoran Desert...Designed for your active lifestyle...A distinctively styled collection of homes... Draped with lush greens and rolling fairways...Miles of walking paths and hiking trails." Lowly subdivisions had been upgraded to "master-planned communities." Add gates to the subdivision and it became even more alluring. The city grew on glowing articles in the newspaper about Phoenix leading the nation in job creation and in attracting Californians who were cashing out the equity in their houses and moving here. Other words were less welcome: the occasional warning of a real-estate bubble or threat to water supplies, the regular reports that showed per-capita income was below the national average, that most of the jobs being created paid badly, and Phoenix lacked the diverse economy needed for a big city to compete. No, this was a story about promise and hope, floated on thirty-year mortgages or ARMs. It was the American Dream. The people who moved in didn't remember the citrus groves or desert that the houses replaced, and they didn't miss what they couldn't recall.

Lindsey came home on the evening of July 3. We are not a couple that meets at curbside. So when I saw her walk past the security checkpoint, in her black jeans and black top and luminous smile, I set aside all my fears and misgivings to just feel her in my arms again. This was the woman I knew. Once again, our talk was easy and comfortable, as if we'd never been apart. Then we went home, to a room lit only by a candle and the cool kiss of the air conditioning on our warm skin. Robin wasn't around, and she found little space in our happy conversation. The newspaper was full of crisis: one of two pipelines that brought gasoline to the city had broken, and gas lines were already appearing at the pumps. Seven homeless people were dead in one day from the one-hundred-seventeen-degree heat. A shootout between rival immigrant smugglers left two children dead. But for a few hours, my life was nothing but right.

When the phone rang later, it pulled me out of such a deep sleep that at first I had the consciousness of a houseplant. By the time Lindsey handed me the receiver, I was awake enough to hear the voice of a sheriff's office dispatcher, and she was telling me where to go.

"What is it, Dave?" Lindsey asked, looking sleepy and freshly ravished. It was a nice look for her.

"I'm supposed to meet Patrick Blair," I said. "All she said was it's related to a 901-H." That was the radio code for homicide. In a two-cop household, you use jargon without even realizing it.

Fifteen minutes later, I was waiting in the deserted parking lot of Park Central, the former shopping center turned offices half a mile north of our house. The temperature seemed to have dropped below one hundred, so I lowered the air conditioning off high/max. There was no crime scene, no flashing lights. But this was where the dispatcher said Blair would meet me. I turned off the lights and sat. Leave it to Blair to ruin my romantic evening. I looked around the deserted lot. When I was a kid, this was the biggest retail center in the state besides downtown. Now all the stores had moved out, and Phoenix had all the big city retail ambiance of Fargo. My bicycle had been stolen at Park Central when I was nine, my first encounter with crime. I couldn't say that put me on a path to become a sheriff's deputy. But there I was, having historical thoughts—or at least the memories that come from moving back to the neighborhood where you grew up. All these thoughts were helping me avoid wondering why Patrick Blair had called me out in the middle of the night.

Middle-of-the-night anxieties weren't long in coming. What about Robin's information that Blair had been in Washington at the same time that Lindsey was there? A man she liked and defended, an old beau perhaps. She had given me no reason to mistrust her. Robin was playing a game. I wanted to think so, but the nervous shaking of my right leg indicated otherwise. Maybe Lindsey's passionate return to me had been fueled by guilt. Maybe that night with Robin I had been angry enough with Lindsey to earn some guilt myself. I could still feel the distinct contours of Robin's breasts against me. I shook my head, hard. What the hell would Dr. Sharon say? She'd say I was tired and acting silly.

To the west, I saw the landing lights of a helicopter, bringing some poor soul into the trauma center at St. Joseph's Hospital. I glanced over at the hospital's rooftop helipad, which already held two choppers. Soon the rotor noise and lights were insistently in my face. Then the Prelude's windows were vibrating and the car was being rocked by rotor wash. I had just enough time to imagine a medical helicopter crashing on the asphalt in front of me, when the chopper descended to a level where I could see the sheriff's star and insignia on the side. Then it was on the ground, a compact steel insect with some kind of jet stabilizer that eliminated the need for a tail rotor. It sent out a wave of gritty dust, and when the rotors stopped a man stepped out and motioned me over.

"What's up, Blair?"

"Sorry to get you out," he said, with just the solicitous manner of someone who had cuckolded me. I tried to put that aside. He asked, "You know a kid who lives in a school bus, out near Hyder?"

"Yeah, he calls himself Davey Crockett. He was near Louie Bell's trailer, gave me the description of the guy in the Dodge truck who might have been…"

Blair's look stopped me. He said, "The kid's dead. Homicide. Tony's already out there. It's apparently pretty bad. The sheriff wants us both out there as soon as possible."

We were already walking to the helicopter. The air took on the scent of aviation fuel.

I had not been a passenger in what was called "Peralta's air force," and given my unease even in an airliner, I had no desire to go. But damned if I would let Patrick Blair know it. So I gamely boarded, and took a seat in the back, pulling the harnesses tight. Blair retook his seat beside the pilot, the engines loudly engaged, and we quickly lifted off. It was too loud to talk. We went straight up, shimmied a little and turned southwest. I held onto the seat, feeling vaguely dizzy as every air pocket and wind gust seemed magnified by the small airframe. I was steady, though. As had been true since I was young, real crisis calmed me. It was only in silence, in repose, what most people called "peace," that I was vulnerable.

I recalled Davey Crockett's small, fragile face and imagined what we might find. Out the window, the world was sharply divided between dark and light. A dense galaxy of city lights flowed out beyond the horizon. But we were low enough to make out the details on skyscrapers—the window-washing rig sat on the top of the Viad Tower—and the red and green of traffic lights. Low-riders chased their headlight beams along McDowell Road. In the distance came the telltale talisman flash of red TV tower lights on the South Mountains. After a few minutes, we left the center of the galaxy and what remained were a few arms of stars that were subdivisions, and finally the wayward outlying solar systems of the few remaining farmers' lights. Then we were in darkness. It was a moonless night and the earth was void. I could only imagine the empty desert below as we felt the updrafts from the mountains. Now light came from real stars above. It was a shame we couldn't just ride in the night and enjoy the view.

We touched down on the road a ways from the Bell trailer, and walked toward the old school bus that had been Davey's home. It was lit up like a movie location set at night, and the characters moving about were all wearing the tan uniforms of the MCSO. I walked beside Blair, hooking my star over my belt like a real cop.

"How was your trip to Washington?" I asked him.

"What are you talking about?" he said. I couldn't see his face in the darkness. He continued, "The only trip I've had in the past year was one to bring back a murderer from Yuma."

By that time, we had reached a perimeter of yellow tape and uniformed deputies. Tony Snyder, Blair's male model Bobbsey Twin partner, met us with latex gloves on his hands. He was drinking out of a liter-sized bottle of Arrowhead water. I was instantly feeling dehydrated.

"His brains are beaten out all over the inside of that school bus," Snyder said. "Roof, windows, floor. It's a hell of a fucking mess. My wife wanted me to look at new houses later today, and I'm on brain cleanup detail." We stood looking at the bus. Its long side faced the road, but was set back maybe fifty feet. It had been decades since it had been painted, but you could make out CASA GRANDE SCHOOLS on the side. Snyder was still talking: "Whoever did it was interrupted. There's all these old hippies who live out here. Guy drives by and hears screaming coming from the bus. So he stops and yells, 'Hey, you all right in there?' Somebody from inside takes a shot at him, so he high-tails it to Hyder and gets some buddies. They call us and come back with guns. But by then, it's too late. What a mess. We're looking for a pipe or something like that, whatever was used to beat him."

"You won't find it," I said. "And it wasn't a pipe. It was a sap."

"A what?"

"A blackjack."

"How do you…?"

I was about to tell him when I heard Peralta's heavy, even tread.

# Chapter Twenty-Six

The sheriff walked with us toward the school bus. He was wearing black slacks and a black polo shirt that blended him in with the desert night. As we walked into the bright floodlights, I could see the anger percolating at the sides of his large eyes. He ignored Blair and Snyder, walking with a meaty hand on my shoulder.

"Mapstone, the responding officers found the victim's wallet. He had a driver's license, a debit card, twenty-two dollars, a picture of his mom, and a sheriff's office business card with your name on it." We paused a few feet from the school bus door, where untold numbers of children had once climbed aboard. "Why did he have your card, Mapstone?"

I looked around. The scene was a mess. The hippie rescuers had ruined any chance to get shoe imprints when they boarded the bus. Now the inside was floodlit, and I could see evidence technicians moving slowly from the rear. The seats were mostly gone, replaced by a bed, an old sofa, a table with a hotplate, and stacks of water bottles. Ah, the simple life in rural Arizona. Snyder hadn't been exaggerating the worst. I saw two skinny legs, pushing out of dusty pants. The wheelchair was tossed aside below the bus steps. The faded vinyl seat was folded and dusty. In the background, I heard the chatter of the police radio. Many people were dying in the county tonight, whether in a robbery gone bad or a hospital bed. And I had seen death so many times as a young deputy. There was no logical reason that the death of this young man named Davey Crockett should mean more to me than any other. But a part of me wanted to cry.

I explained things to Peralta, who kept muttering under his breath, "what about the book, Mapstone…you were supposed to be working on a book." I just talked over him. I could see the alarmed looks on young deputies and evidence techs.

"So," Peralta said, "you put a civilian in danger."

"I didn't put him in danger," I said testily. My insides weren't so sure. I felt a wave of nausea. I swallowed heavily and made my best case, to Peralta and to my gathering guilty conscience. "He told me he felt safe. He told me the man in the truck hadn't seen him spying on the Bell brothers. I wrote all this up and forwarded it to the detectives, and to the tribal police. I did my part, and then I went back to your book." I emphasized the "your."

"So what's your hypothesis?" he said mildly.

I gave it to him as best I could. Some of it just had to be improvised. "The tattooed guy in the Dodge truck appeared to be intimidating Louie Bell. That was what Davey thought. He seems a more likely suspect for the casino murder than the pickpocket. We know he came back and went through the Bell trailer after Louie was murdered. But he still wasn't satisfied. He was looking for something, or worried that Davey had seen him. So he came back earlier tonight."

Blair added, "Or maybe the kid surprised him over at the Bell trailer again, and he followed him back to the school bus."

"Go check that trailer," Peralta ordered.

"There's something else," I said. "I've seen this man with the big tattoo on his arm." I told Peralta about the night at El Pedregal, and the woman I was intending to meet.

His jaw tightened but he said nothing.

"The inside of the bus was pretty trashed," Snyder said. "Somebody was taking the place apart looking for something."

I looked over Peralta's shoulder. "Has anybody looked in there?" I pointed to the compartment built into the side of the bus. Blair and Snyder looked at each other, then we all walked over. Snyder gave it a couple of strong pulls and the metal door fell open. A flashlight showed rusty tools, old rags, an ancient jack, and a bulky, legal-sized envelope.

Thirty minutes later, after the envelope had been photographed, logged into the chain of custody, and gone through other hoops designed to foil clever defense attorneys, its contents were spread out on the hood of a sheriff's office SUV. I had gone from wide-awake to wired to fading in the course of a couple of hours. My body wasn't twenty years old anymore, although Lindsey had made me feel that way a few hours before. The contents of the envelope didn't contribute to my alertness. It looked like the kind of papers you might get at a house closing. Then I saw a name.

"Holy…"

Peralta and the Bobbseys crowded around. Everybody was sweating but Peralta. The sheriff demanded to know if I was wearing gloves.

"I didn't just fall off the turnip truck," I grumped. My fingers were leafing through legal documents. I walked them through.

"This is a deed transfer for a piece of property in Maricopa County. The grantor is Louis Bell. The grantees are Tom and Dana Earley."

"The supervisor?" Snyder said.

I nodded. Peralta said, "We don't know that. It's a common name."

"Not when it's Tom married to a woman named Dana," I said. "And look, here's their address in Gilbert. It's the same guy." I flipped pages. "But look. It was never signed by Bell, never filed."

"What property is it?" Peralta asked, pushing closer to the documents on the SUV hood. "You'll have to go online. Maybe go down to the plat books at the county."

"I already know the plat number," I said. "It's the Bell land west of Tonopah."

"Where the old guy wanted to be buried," Snyder said.

Peralta had a letter in his hands. I read over his shoulder. It was from the Earleys' lawyer. "They had a tentative deal, and then Bell refused to sign," Peralta said. It was dated two weeks before Louie Bell was murdered.

"I know what you're thinking, Mapstone," he said. "Stop."

I leafed through the other contents of the legal-sized envelope. If there was any doubt remaining, there were two Tom Earley business cards. One in his role as president of Earley Development Group, and the other as Maricopa County supervisor. A color brochure of the Arizona Dreams development was stapled to another business card, for someone named Shelley Baker. On a single sheet of legal paper the name Earl Rice was written in pencil, and underlined.

"Look at this." Blair was talking. He pointed to the signature of the lawyer for Louis Bell, at the bottom of the deed transfer. My spine expanded at least an inch: the name was Alan Cordesman, and the date of the document was a month before he was found murdered in Willo.

"We need a warrant tonight," Blair said. "We've got to get access to the Earley house before they realize we know, and start destroying evidence."

"Wait," Peralta said.

"Earley and his wife are connected to three homicides by these documents," Blair said. "This is what the suspect was looking for. Bell probably gave this to Davey Crockett for safekeeping. Earley clearly had a financial interest…"

"No," Peralta said.

"Blair's right," I said quietly. Deputies were crowded around us, nervously fingering their leather belt accessories, snapping and unsnapping items in the timeless fidgeting of cops. Peralta glared at me. "I want that evidence sealed for now," he said. "Mapstone, you can go."

I didn't move. He glared at me more. His face would have been at home among the heads on Easter Island. It didn't intimidate me. We had been patrol deputies in another life, and I claimed some prerogatives of a former partner. I looked him back in the eye. No one spoke. After what seemed like five minutes, he said, "Talk to me over here for a minute," and stalked out to the road.

Then he walked fast out into the night. I had to trot at first to keep up. The air was cooler than in the city, and as we gained distance from the floodlights, the canopy of stars emerged. Grand eternity enveloped us, courtesy of the dry atmosphere. On the earth, we might as well have been a hundred miles from even a drink of water. The empty land cascaded outward in every direction, contained only by the eerie black shapes of mountains and buttes that occluded the fantastic constellations and billions of distant suns that lit our walk.

"Tell me a historical story, Mapstone," Peralta said. "That's what you're supposed to be here for."

"You'd be bored." I was all out of history for the moment. Davey Crockett was dead and the Alamo had fallen.

We walked on in silence. Finally, I said, "We're not too far from the site of the Oatman massacre. It was 1851, I think. An Apache war party attacked a group of settlers headed for California. A little girl named Olive Oatman was kidnapped. She was later sold to the Mohave Indians, and then…"

"What have you gotten us into, Mapstone?"

He didn't wait for me to answer.

"This man is a very powerful politician," he said.

"You're the most powerful politician in the county," I said.

"Times change," he replied.

"What do you mean times change?"

"Mapstone, look at who's running the country. People like Tom Earley. These are the kind of people that don't sweat when they fuck. Understand? But I have to get along with them."

I stopped and stared at him. I could only see the wide planes of his face illuminated by starlight. "Are you telling me you're afraid to investigate this?"

"I am afraid," he said. "But it doesn't matter. This is political dynamite. Even if I decided the evidence was worth looking at, I'd have to turn it over to another law enforcement agency. DPS or the Pima County sheriff. There can't be any charge of conflict of interest."

"The Earleys aren't above the law," I protested. "Dana came to me with a fake letter from a fake father. Then she claimed she was being blackmailed. When I asked for the evidence, she wanted to meet at El Pedregal. I nearly got my brains beaten in, and she never called me again. And all you can talk about is politics?"

"Go home," he ordered.

"What the hell is wrong with you?" I erupted. "These documents link together three separate murders. When have you ever been cautious or political? You're not. It's why people respect you and love you. Something is going on. My office was broken into. The lock was knocked out clean as surgery. Who did that, in a guarded county building, and what were they looking for? Last time I checked you were the sheriff. And now you want to go hide behind protocol?"

"You're out of line."

"I know. But I'm right."

"You sound like Sharon."

I kicked at the sandy dirt, just to be kicking something. "You had a good thing going there, and you screwed it up. I know, I'm out of line."

"She wanted to move on," he said. "I was holding her back."

I let it be. I said, "Why don't you let Blair and Snyder look into this."

"I can see the headline," Peralta said. "SHERIFF INVESTIGATES POWERFUL POLITICIAN WHO IS CRITIC OF DEPARTMENT."

"So let me quietly look into it," I said.

"No."

"Give me a few days."

He repeated, "No."

I was tired and angry, and I was rapidly pushing through the boundaries that even old partners respect. "Damn you," I said. "That young man back there was abandoned by everybody in the world. When he fell off a roof while he was working for his father, his dad cut him loose. God, I hate what Arizona has become. And now he can't expect justice from the Maricopa

County sheriff." I finished and bit my lip and stared out at a mass that I believed was Fourth of July Peak. It was now the Fourth of July, three in the morning. Peralta just grunted.

He asked, "What ever happened to the little girl who was kidnapped?"

"What? Oh, Olive Oatman? She was eventually rescued. She lived into her sixties."

"How could wagon trains have come through here? It's so barren and dry."

"They followed the Gila River and there were a few wells along the way. It was very difficult. Stop changing the subject."

Peralta started walking back toward the scene. "Get back to the book, Mapstone. It'll be good for you."

"What if I do other things on my own time?" I asked. "Check out some names. You don't need to know anything. I'm just the crazy professor, working on his own."

"No," he snarled. "And I mean goddamned no!"

I let him stalk ahead. He got about ten feet and stopped, just standing there, his back toward me, his broad shoulders rigid with tension. Out into the night he said, "It might take a few days to sort everything out here. I'd say four days. You know how this damned bureaucracy works."

He turned back to me and said, "Take Lindsey with you." Then he walked on. A few more steps, and I heard, "And don't be stupid." All in all, I took that as permission from the sheriff.

Then he walked into the floodlights, and I followed to bum a ride back to the city. It was Independence Day, after all.

# Chapter Twenty-Seven

The next day, Tuesday, Lindsey and I gassed up her Prelude at the county pumps downtown and drove to north Scottsdale. The alternative was to prowl the streets looking for an open gas station, then sit in line for an hour. That was what most people were doing. The morning's newspaper said it would be several days before the pipeline could be repaired. Until then, trucks were bringing in some gas from Tucson. People were learning that Phoenix was the nation's fifth largest city in population only; it didn't have a refinery, or very convenient mass transit.

Even with the shortages, traffic was heavy and tense, in the high summer way, and the air was filthy. Heat and tailpipe exhaust radiated up from the wide streets as we drove and I filled Lindsey in on the case. As usual, she asked the right questions, some I hadn't thought about. At stoplights, when my eyes could stray from the road, I watched her, trying out my new eyes, the ones Robin had implanted while she was drunkenly wrapped around me. Maybe Robin had lied about Blair going to Washington, but what about Lindsey being a teenage mother? If it were true, it wouldn't change anything in how I adored her. Even though the woman who claimed she trusted me with everything hadn't trusted me with the biggest event of her life. To Robin, it was a sign Lindsey still wanted her bad boy, the father, and I was only a temporary safe harbor. None of it might be true, but those new eyes still scratched and irritated. In an hour, we reached the Scottsdale Airpark and the offices of the Arizona Dreams development.

The airpark had been the trendy corporate address for several years. Top executives could fly in and own a house in the McDowell Mountains, but otherwise keep Phoenix at arms' length. Employees were priced out of Scottsdale, so they were forced to commute from miles away, from places like Chandler and Surprise and Glendale. The result was to make the low-density, rich paradise of Scottsdale into a sieve for the worst traffic jams in the Valley. It helped cook the smog that obscured the purple-gray undulations of the McDowells off to the northeast. The buildings weren't much to look at, either: just dull, off-the-shelf two- and three-story tilt-up jobs found in every office park in America. They were surrounded by sidewalks that went nowhere and rock landscaping that radiated the morning heat like a convection oven. Nobody seemed to care, as more buildings went up every year.

We walked past a security guard reading a comic book—he looked about thirty—to a building directory listing nothing but builders, mortgage companies, land advisers, and Arizona Dreams LLC. Things kept coming back to this housing development. Dana Earley was the voice in their ubiquitous radio ads. I could almost recite by rote their promise of a return to real neighborhoods and genuine small-town living. Then the brochure found in the belly of the old school bus, secreted away with papers that Louis Bell might have given Davey Crockett for safekeeping. Papers so sensitive that somebody was willing to kill to find them. And the business card of Shelley Baker. We were coming without making an appointment. The building air was frigid, and felt good on my superheated skin. Lindsey, wearing a dark paisley skirt and white top, looked as fresh as morning in a place where the surface temperatures could reach one hundred forty degrees.

The company's suite was not nearly so lax about security. The entry doors led you to a reception desk with standard-issue pleasant young woman. But off to the side was a waist-high partition, behind which sat a pair of serious-looking and well conditioned young men. Think Army Special Forces. They scowled at me.

They even scowled at Lindsey. But they lost interest when we showed our badges and asked to see Ms. Baker. While we waited, there was the scale model to keep us busy. It took up a table that looked the size of our bedroom and was protected by a Plexiglas shell. Inside were hundreds of tiny houses on curvy streets, golf courses, hiking trails, and desert preserve. The legend said Arizona Dreams would be one of the largest master-planned communities in the state's history. At build-out, in 2020, it was to have 40,000 houses. I tried to imagine why Louis Bell, desert rat who lived in a trailer, would want anything to do with it. The project would go west of the White Tank Mountains, a mountain range away from the Salt River Valley. But it would still be miles east of the Bell property.

Just then a tall woman in a red suit came out and introduced herself as Shelley.

"Expecting trouble?" Lindsey nodded toward the muscle cubicle.

"Oh," Shelley Baker said, "there have been threats from environmentalists."

I figured there were about three environmentalists in Arizona, and they had contractor's licenses. But I took her word for it as she led us past an inner door and down a hallway of offices to a conference room. Out the windows were the slopes of the McDowell Mountains. Running up to them were some of the priciest houses in town. I remembered going out there to target shoot as a teenager, when it had all been virgin desert. Now there was probably a kid who was doing the same thing in the empty desert west of the White Tank Mountains, and someday, when it's chock-a-block with tract houses, he might remember.

Baker was talking. "This isn't really the Arizona Dreams sales office. We will open that next month, along with several models." We sat and she faced us. "But that's not why you're here."

I put her around fifty, with honey-colored hair worn swept back and good features, as angular as an ironing board. The sun, of course, had done its work. Her hair was as dried as hay. Her tan was the texture and color of a saddlebag. But her face looked frozen into a perpetual look of happy curiosity—and people pay big money for these face-lifts. Maybe she was really pushing seventy, and I shouldn't be so critical. I told her there wasn't much I could tell her. Her business card had been found at a crime scene, a homicide. I told her where. Nothing registered on her taut skin.

"I've never even been there," she said. "People can get business cards anywhere."

Lindsey said, "Your card didn't say what you do for the company."

"I'm the general counsel," she said.

"So your card might not be available to just anybody trying to buy a house," I said.

"That's kind of argumentative, Deputy…"

"Mapstone," I said. She noted it on a legal pad in front of her, and when her eyes settled on me again they were paying attention.

I thought about Davey Crockett, abandoned in the desert by his sleazebag contractor father, only to be beaten to death. Lindsey could sense my anger, and gave me a subtle look. It said, *Be calm, Dave.* So I swallowed hard and asked Baker for information on the owners of Arizona Dreams.

"It's an LLC, a limited liability company. We're not required to disclose our partners. Unless, of course, you have something from the court. Do you?"

"Not yet," I said.

"I didn't think so," she said. "This kind of an entity is established in part for the privacy of the corporate structure and ownership. But you wouldn't be disappointed. These are big names, respected people. We're capitalized as well as any master-planned community in the West. And every major homebuilder has signed on, all national names. This is big business, deputies."

"It does sound impressive," Lindsey said.

"It is," Baker said. "You really ought to consider buying at Arizona Dreams. There are special communities there for professionals like law enforcement and teachers…"

"Who are paid badly," Lindsey said.

"But who deserve the best in a community," Baker came right back. It was startling to see the sales pitch kick in, even for the general counsel. "My husband and I have been out, and seen the sweet spot of the development, right in the foothills where the Sierra Montana clubhouse will be. We decided right then to buy out there. What part of town do you live in?"

Lindsey volunteered, "We both live in the Willo Historic District, north of downtown."

Baker drew in a breath. "I don't know anyone who would live there."

I was tempted to say the same about her suburban sprawl. I asked, "Who do you work for, Ms. Baker?"

"I work for Jared Malkin. He's our managing partner." The face still looked happy to see me. The eyes definitely weren't.

"Is Mr. Malkin in?"

"No," she said. "He's at a business meeting in Malibu. But I can speak for the entire company on this matter. Lots of people have literature from Arizona Dreams. Even, apparently, your unfortunate victim. But dreaming about a great master-planned community is no crime, Deputy Mapstone."

I watched her in silence to see if she really believed the sales jargon she was spouting. That damned frozen face again. It was stuck open like a garage door. I said, "The crime is a young man beaten to death. Have you ever seen anyone beaten to death, Ms. Baker?"

She stared at me sternly, but her face drained of its saddlebag tan.

"I don't see…" she started.

"Your card was at this crime scene, Ma'am," I said, in my best patrol deputy voice. "Not the card of a Realtor, or subcontractor, but you, the general counsel of Arizona Dreams. Why was your card there?"

I expected her to lash back at me. But she just sat there. Her right index finger tapped quietly on the dark wood of the conference table. I was tempted to look at the beauty of the mountains out the windows. But I kept staring at her.

I asked, in a quiet, even voice, "Ever hear of Louis or Harry Bell?"

"No," she said.

"They were landowners west of Tonopah," I shot back.

"I don't know them." She was speaking through gritted teeth, like someone impersonating a Clint Eastwood character. "We would have had no interest in property that far out."

I asked, "Alan Cordesman?"

She pursed her lips and shook her head.

"How about Earl Rice?"

She kept shaking the head. "As I say, I'm afraid I just can't help you. Do you realize what Arizona Dreams is? If not, I may have to fire our marketing person." Her mouth and cheeks struggled to turn their surgical smile into a genuine insincere smile. "This is a project unlike any Arizona has ever seen. We'll be the size of a small city…"

We were getting nowhere when Lindsey said, "Well, you must feel pretty good having Dana Earley…"

Shelley Baker said quickly, "As I say, there's nothing I can disclose about our investors." And her right cheek twitched. As we walked out into the lobby, workmen had removed the plastic dome over the giant model of Arizona Dreams, no doubt to add more houses.

# Chapter Twenty-Eight

We walked out into the blast furnace of a morning. I'm usually not a fast walker, but I felt Lindsey take my hand to slow me down.

"Dave, are you okay?"

"Sure," I said.

"Dave." She stopped me and took both my hands. "You're not okay. And if you don't want to talk about it right now, that's okay, too. I'm just a little concerned. You seemed angry in there..."

"I just hate the summer," I lied, and kissed her, which was no lie. A pair of office workers walked by and smiled. I smiled at Lindsey. Even in the intense sunlight, her eyes were their usual soothing dark blue.

She said, "We'll reschedule that trip, Dave. I promise. I'm sorry. Don't be angry."

"I'm not mad at you," I said, and stroked her soft hair. My hand caught on plastic. A tiny headphone.

"Sorry," she said. "You're married to gadget girl."

I stroked her face and we walked to the car. I wasn't lying: I do hate Phoenix in the summer. I just wasn't being completely honest. I wasn't mad at Lindsey, really. It was Robin who had planted this ugly feeling in me. The secret child, unrevealed by the woman who claimed she could tell me anything. The old boyfriend who still had the power to move her unlike any other man. The sister who carried this news like a Typhoid Mary, and yet for a moment I was kissing her back, willing to walk on that wild side. An ugly feeling, made in the kiln of late-night insomnia. It was powerful enough to crack through all the walls that adults painstakingly build around primal emotions. It surprised me and scared me. David Mapstone, sophisticated intellectual, was just as insecure and jealous as the next guy. All of it was made worse in the echo chamber of my thoughts—but I was uncharacteristically wary of raising any of it with Lindsey. I hated revisionist history when it got personal.

We waited for the air conditioning to cool the inside of the car, and Lindsey asked for a shady spot so she could see her computer screen. It was no easy task. New Phoenix buildings were there to make money, not waste it on shade structures or rediscovering the cool spaces of old Spanish or Moorish architecture. Even in tony north Scottsdale every surface was exposed, and the only trees were ineffective palo verdes. I finally found a building to hide behind, the sun went away, and the temperature seemed to drop ten degrees.

"I'm always afraid this will melt," she said, retrieving her laptop computer from its case stashed behind the passenger seat. "Let's find out about Earl Rice. All you have is a name?"

"Yes, it was written on a piece of paper that was along with the stash in the school bus."

"I could do more with a Social Security number," she said, opening the laptop and booting it up.

"Can't you find it with all your government spy stuff?"

"Oh, Dave," she said. "Now I have to kill you. But for you, it will be the *petit mort.*" She rubbed a hand across my thigh. "This is just my regular G-4 Mac. I can't use the super-duper stuff for mere sheriff's work. They monitor every keystroke, and I'd be no fun in a federal prison."

I rubbed her neck while she typed.

"Oh, God, I missed that while I was in Washington," she sighed. "This is interesting. Earl Rice is a hydrologist, and it just so happens he did some work for Arizona Dreams LLC. He's listed in their prospectus. Hang on. Wireless reception sucks up here…"

While we waited we talked about the house, the stray cats of Willo, the next book we would read to each other now that she was back. It was comforting, part of our life without Robin, without these new revelations. Then Lindsey said Robin had asked her if she could rent the garage apartment for a few months. She asked me what I thought.

"I don't know," I said slowly, wishing she were gone.

"I don't think it's a good idea," Lindsey said. Then, "Check this out. Rice is listed on documents that Arizona Dreams had to file with the Department of Water Resources, attesting that the land has a 100-year water supply."

"Researching my dissertation would have been a lot more fun with you," I said.

"You probably used dead trees, too," she said. "So there are two things in that envelope that connect to Arizona Dreams—Baker's business card, and Earl Rice's name written down."

"And," I said, "thanks to your brilliant police work, the Earleys are apparently investors in the limited partnership."

"Just luck, my love. Here's another lucky stroke. Rice's office and home are close. The office is right on the south side of the airpark."

She directed me to an address on Seventy-Eighth Place, an older one-story building. Out here, "older" meant from the 1980s. We stepped out to the noise of a Lear jet taking off. But we were back in the car in five minutes. The office was dark and empty, and someone in the neighboring suite, an office of construction defect attorneys, said Rice had retired last year. So we drove again, this time down Scottsdale Road to Shea, then east across the Pima Freeway. Five more minutes, and we found the right cul-de-sac.

Hydrologists must do well, at least based on the Rice house. It was a custom job, with more attention paid to the quality of the stucco and coloring and tile roof. Native stone turrets provided the grand entryway. On the opposite side, another turret had French doors from a patio to a dining room, or maybe a study. The lot was spacious, and shaded by tangly mesquite and cottonwood trees. We pulled into the curving drive, directly in front of the entry. I started out but Lindsey's voice stopped me.

"Dave," she said, handing me my holstered Colt Python. "I know it's hot outside, and you don't like to carry. But someone tried to hurt you, and he may be the same one who murdered three people." I took the gun and she smiled. That smile alone was worth it. We walked up the flagstones to the double front doors, which were painted a glossy black and looked out from darkened, beveled glass. The street was quiet except for a leaf blower, far away. I rang the doorbell, and just out of old habits, habits I had learned in the academy and then had carried with me for years, even as a college professor—out of old habits, I stood aside. Lindsey was already standing on the other side of the door, with the wall to her side.

The explosion of gunfire and shattering of glass came at the same instant. I turned my head away from the wash of shards and watched nickel-sized chunks of wood fly out of the trunk of a mesquite tree. My brain said "automatic weapon," but my body was in charge, crouching down against the wall. The heavy .357 Magnum was in my hand, and I couldn't recall how it got there. Lindsey was in a similar pose on the other side of the doorway, holding her black baby Glock 26 in a two-handed combat grip. The Mapstones, enjoying one of the finer neighborhoods of north Scottsdale.

"Hey!" A bald, tanned man in green shorts was marching our way. "You don't live here!"

"Get away, you idiot!" Lindsey yelled, and another burst of fire sent the man scuttling back behind his wall. My ears were ringing.

"Sheriff's deputies!" I shouted, producing yet another string of gunfire. The poor mesquite was looking quite wounded. "That obviously did a lot of good," I said in a conversational voice.

Lindsey tried to smile at me, but in her eyes I could see that she had done the same calculus that kept me melted against the wall. Neither of us could hope to get on the other side of the Prelude, and relative safety, without a perhaps fatal run across the drive. Moving along the wall was no good, either. The windows could become gun-ports. I kept glancing behind, toward the French doors that opened onto a patio. Aside from the ringing in my ears, it became quiet. Not even the leaf blower was sounding. I cleaved closer to the wall and motioned for Lindsey to get down more.

Sweat sluiced off my sides and back, but I fought to stop shivering. Lindsey produced a cell phone from her bag and held it to her face. A piece of glass clattered out of the door, nearly making me open fire. I pulled the Python back, the four-inch barrel close to my face, reducing my profile as much as possible. The barrel was surprisingly cool. The bulk of the car seemed as far away as Paris. And all my strength was going to tamp down the panic that threatened to engulf me: Lindsey was in danger.

In an instant, something heavy put me on the ground, and the ground seemed to shift for a second. It took my ears and brain a couple seconds more to process what had happened. Something big had blown up. It sounded like it had come from the back of the house. A nauseating chemical smell was in the air. Lindsey was still crouched, leaning against the far wall, safe. Then, in the distance, sirens.

It was only a few hours of report writing and a cautionary visit to the emergency room, and even that didn't yield Earl Rice. As the Scottsdale cops explained it, Rice had sold the house the previous winter, and an investor in Minneapolis had bought it. The renters were cooking meth and protecting it with automatic weapons. They blew the place when they thought we were raiding it. The cops didn't ask much about what we were doing there once it became clear we weren't narcotics detectives trying to steal a showy bust in their town. Peralta never arrived. By the time we left Scottsdale Police Headquarters, the sun was far in the west and the air was broiling with heat and dust.

We had celebratory martinis at Z-Tejas with the fashionable Scottsdale crowd, all the rapturous bodies and perfect tans. Then we ate Thai food at Malee's on Main. Peralta's deadline was glaring at us with the same intensity as his obsidian eyes, but for a few hours it was just good to celebrate being alive, and being alive with my love. When we left Scottsdale it was full dark. Although the heat was unbearable, at least the sun was gone for a few hours. We drove back home through light mid-week traffic on Indian School Road.

This soothing streetlight contentment in me lasted until I caught sight of the police cruisers in front of our house.

# Chapter Twenty-Nine

The front door was standing open to Cypress Street, a fortune in air-conditioning being lost. We identified ourselves to a uniformed officer on the porch. He led us inside, where Robin was sitting on the leather sofa, her blond mane more disheveled than usual. Kate Vare was standing behind her with a satisfied look on her thin face.

"David!" Robin leapt up and grabbed me, kissing me on the mouth before I could push her away. "You've got to stop them!" she pleaded. I didn't notice if she hugged Lindsey, because soon Vare and a couple of the uniforms were pulling her back onto the sofa.

"Kate…" I began.

"We're executing a search warrant, Mapstone," she said. "Please sit down."

"I think we'll stand," Lindsey said. Her voice was small and dry. "Let me see the warrant."

Vare held out an envelope and Lindsey took it. She put on her glasses, read it slowly, then handed it to me. I started to read it, but Lindsey was advancing on Kate. "That warrant includes computers and contents, and I'm calling the sheriff and the U.S. attorney. My laptops contain highly…"

"Don't get your knickers twisted, missy," Vare said.

"My name is Lindsey."

Vare went on. "We haven't even looked in the main part of the house. We didn't need to."

Coldness crept into my middle. None of the old familiar surroundings gave me any comfort.

"You read all those books, Mapstone?" Vare waved toward the floor-to-ceiling shelves at the north end of the living room.

"They're just for show, Kate. What cold case has brought you to our house?"

"There's no cold case, Mapstone," she said. "I'm just helping out the homicide detectives…"

"She's trying to make it like I murdered Al!" Robin blurted in a loud, choked voice. Her face was red and tears were streaming down. Lindsey slowly moved to her, stood next to her and stroked her hair. "He gave it to me! He gave it to me…"

"You've been advised of your rights, Miss Deller," Vare said.

"Deller?" I said.

"Keep quiet, Robin," Lindsey said, and stroked her head. Robin lolled her head against Lindsey's hip, like a child. Lindsey looked at me intently, and I knew at least one message she was telegraphing was, I thought Robin's last name was Bryson.

Robin said quietly, "David, help me."

Vare went outside with me, reluctantly.

I wheeled on her. "What the hell are you doing?"

"My job."

"This isn't your job. This woman is Lindsey's sister. She works as an art curator in Paradise Valley. She's been living with us for the past two months. She's got nothing to do with a homicide."

"Do you have feelings for her, Mapstone? None of my business, I guess." Kate's expression was unreadable. "Some of what you said may be true. But she was Alan Cordesman's girlfriend at the time he was killed."

"She was living with some guy named Edward."

"So she had another man on the side. The only one I care about is Cordesman. Two people down at Paisley Violin identified her with him late on the night of February 11, the night before the Willo home tour."

Now that cold feeling in my chest was deep winter.

"That was five months ago, Kate. Why didn't you show up with an arrest warrant five months ago?"

Her mouth narrowed. "I don't owe you an explanation, Mapstone. Let's just say I did a more thorough job than the detectives back in February."

"This is bullshit."

Vare crossed her arms smugly. "Your sister-in-law has a rap sheet. Did you know that? Not good for the image of the sheriff's office. Petty theft. Bad checks. Possession. That last one sent her away for six months in Colorado. This was before tough drug sentencing, lucky for her. I make her out for some kind of addict and con."

"Did you find drugs?" I demanded.

I saw Vare's teeth flash like a predator's. "No. I found better. I found this."

She dangled a small plastic evidence envelope. I took it reluctantly.

"That ring matches the photos from Cordesman's insurance records. It was his mother's wedding ring."

"Maybe," I said.

"Mapstone," she cut me off. "That ring was the only thing missing from Alan Cordesman's house the day somebody rammed an ice pick into his brain."

"Now wait..."

"I found that ring in your sister-in-law's room, in your garage apartment."

I said, "Kate, this is nuts. I can't explain everything about Robin, but we're working on something that's going to tie up Cordesman and..."

"Look, you son of a bitch," she hissed. "I think that some-body who rammed an ice pick into Alan Cordesman's brain was Robin, and I've got the evidence to make a case. It's only a matter of time before we find why she would have done the same thing to the old man in the casino. She's going downtown as a material witness while we talk to the county attorney. And you—you're lucky we don't toss your whole house, and take you both into custody for harboring a fugitive. I bet you knew, you son of a bitch…"

I moved out of her way. "Thanks for the professional courtesy, sergeant."

"Out of professional courtesy," she said, "you and Lindsey aren't going downtown, too."

# Chapter Thirty

Little things. In retrospect, I should have wondered more about them. Robin was an art student without art books or art. The garage apartment had remained nearly as bare as the day she moved in. She had come back to Phoenix because a rich man in Paradise Valley wanted her expertise in WPA-era art. Where were her Social Realism posters? Why had she never mentioned the restored WPA murals in the old downtown Post Office? I was afraid to find out if she really worked for this rich man, or if a boyfriend named Edward ever existed. We walked with Robin to the curb. The streetlight illuminated tracks of spent tears. Bend down. Watch your head. Swing your legs in. The prisoner section of patrol cars is cramped and smelly, the seat invariably sticky. The cars drove west on Cypress, then their taillights swung onto Fifth Avenue toward downtown and disappeared into the night.

When I stepped inside the door and closed it, Lindsey turned on me, a furious light in her eyes.

"Did you fuck my sister?!" she screamed, and gave me a hard, line-of-scrimmage shove.

She screamed again, "Did you fuck Robin? You did, didn't you! You fucked her!" She battered my shoulder with her fists. "God, I knew you would! I knew it!"

The woman standing before me was a stranger, a snarling bully who seemed capable of any cruelty. "You fucked Robin!" she screamed again. She rammed her arms toward me again, and I caught them, as gently as I could. I was saying "no," but her eyes told me she wasn't listening. For a moment, we wrestled arms and hands. Lindsey shrieked half words and obscenities. This banshee's face flushed a vivid red, something close to murder in her eyes. She was also strong as hell. I tried to pull her close, to hug her, calm her down. She pulled away and one hand cuffed me sharply on the right cheekbone. It was enough to break the rhythm of rage.

"Oh!" she moaned. "Oh, Dave, oh, baby…I hurt you…"

"I'm okay," I said, unconsciously backing away. My cheek throbbed, my breath came rapidly and I was tamping down my own surprise. And anger. The whole room seemed alien and hostile. It was a feeling that lasted until she took my hands. We ended up on the couch, and for a long time she just clung to me and cried. I looked at us a couple of times, reflected in the picture window. For a few minutes my watchful, poetic lover had been annihilated, and someone else was there. I let my eyes search for answers in the vaulted ceiling. I only found a couple of spider webs.

"Lindsey," I finally said. "I want to tell you what happened with Robin…"

She shook her head adamantly. "Later. Not now. Just forgive me and love me…"

"I do," I said. "There's nothing to forgive…Robin and I…"

"No," she said. "Don't. Just forgive me."

I assured her, but I'm not sure if she was really listening. She seemed elsewhere, as if she might just drift away if I weren't hanging on tightly.

"I heard Linda's voice coming out of my mouth," Lindsey said. "I heard her yelling, just now. It was just as vivid as if I were twelve years old, and listening to her fight with her boyfriend, or me or Robin for wanting to stay out. But it was me, my voice. Oh, my God…"

I stroked her dark, straight-as-a-pin hair, pushed it back from her face.

"I can't believe Robin could kill someone," she went on. "But I don't know anything. Look what people do when they're crazy on meth or something else. She was such a sweet little girl…I didn't like what she became as a teenager. I thought I saw all Linda's bad traits in her. Linda's destructiveness. What a fool I was. Linda's bad traits are all in me, too. And I thought I spent my whole life trying to get away from that…Oh, Dave, your poor face…"

"Do you want to go down to the jail? The deputies would make an exception for you."

"No." She shook her head.

"Let's go to bed," I said. "They won't arraign her until the morning. We'll call Peralta. He'll line up a good lawyer."

"I can't sleep," she said. She sat up and looked at me, her eyes a tangle of red. "I really thought I had escaped my upbringing. Then I thought Robin had done the same thing, and I was so proud. It seemed possible. I hadn't seen her in nearly ten years. And on the surface, I thought, 'I've walked away from someone who would drag me down.' But I never stopped hoping that one day, I might be walking down a street, maybe with the man of my dreams, and I would run into Robin, and she would have had a happy ending, too. You must think I am such a fool."

"You're the most sensible person I know," I said. "You changed my life, Lindsey. Everything was different and better after the first time I saw you. In Records. In that black miniskirt."

She smiled at me, that familiar treasured face. She stroked the good side of my face gently.

"So things can change," I said. "I'll never fault you for loving someone and hoping…"

"Let's get out of the house," she said. "Let's just drive. Distract me—now that I've committed spousal battery. Let's go spy on your soccer mom, Dana."

"She lives behind a gate, unfortunately. I'd love to find the hydrologist, Earl Rice."

"No forwarding address," she said. "So what about Jared Malkin, managing partner of Arizona Dreams? You drive, and I'll find his address."

She read out an address in north Scottsdale, so we sailed on rubberized asphalt north on the Piestewa Parkway, rising through the Phoenix Mountain Preserve. Traffic was light. The city looked best at night. The car was quiet except for the tapping of Lindsey's fingers on her keyboard. When we turned east on the 101, Lindsey spoke.

"Here's a story in the *Republic* archives about Jared Malkin. He's fifty-five years old, worked for his old man, who was one of the biggest developers in Orange County. Lucky Sperm Club kid. Had his share of trouble, though. County records show he had two hundred lawsuits against him back in the 1990s over a development in Surprise. He's connected to East Valley Republicans, especially County Supervisor Tom Earley. Lucky again. Did some housing in Gilbert and Chandler. Arizona Dreams is by far his largest project. Major homebuilders, big capital from real estate investment trusts in New York. Sounds like a big shot. I'll save this for you."

"What about arrests?"

"You are so suspicious, Dave. But I already checked. No IRS liens, either. I want to do some snooping on Arizona Dreams LLC. It's not as shut-tight-secret as Miss Battle-Axe thinks. But for now, I've got to give my eyes a break." She shut the machine off, and the cabin of the car fell into darkness as we got off the freeway and made the long drive north on Scottsdale Road.

By the time we were winding through the Desert Mountain area, the gas gauge was below half-full. I hadn't noticed one open gas pump on the way up here.

"God, I hate Scottsdale," she said. "The attack of the plastic pod people. I always feel like the shortest, fattest, poorest person up here. But at least I'm not a plastic pod person."

"Definitely not."

We cruised slowly along streets lined with exquisite desert landscaping, stucco walls, and heavy iron gates. The road rolled here and there with the land to make way for a dry wash. Where they were visible, houses sat back in tasteful spotlights. You could almost feel the aura of conquest. Up here, middle-class was a house that cost two million. But being rich in Arizona wasn't always what it seemed. More than one was unfurnished on the inside except for a card table and a couple of lawn chairs. I was happier in Willo.

"Slow down," Lindsey said. "It's got to be right up here."

For such a big-time developer, he had a smaller house by Desert Mountain standards. But it looked pleasant, a single-story, Santa Fe-style adobe. Two cars sat in the rustic gravel drive, one a gray SUV. And SUVs are so commonplace on the streets of Phoenix, even gray ones called Armadas, that I wouldn't have given it another thought. Except at that very moment—and the dashboard clock said 2:14 a.m.—at that moment, the door to the house opened and a woman with strawberry blond hair walked out. She had an overnight bag in one hand, and the hand of a tall, husky man in the other. Then she turned and gave him a kiss. It wasn't the kind of kiss that business partners exchanged, even in north Scottsdale.

# Chapter Thirty-One

We had a quick breakfast at Susan's Diner and returned to the house in north Scottsdale at eight a.m. The goal was to catch Jared Malkin before he could hide behind the broad-shouldered security men in the lobby of the Arizona Dreams office. It was Wednesday now, and by Peralta's clock we had until Friday to find something that would make this investigation something more than a political hot potato. Another clock was ticking now, too: Robin. She was scheduled to go before a judge today at eleven. So far, we had too many leads and too few answers. John Locke said "the great art of learning is to understand but little at a time." Maybe so, but he never had to deal with Mike Peralta.

After seeing Dana Earley kiss Malkin outside his door, we followed her back to Gilbert. When she pulled into her gated subdivision, we returned home for a few hours of restless sleep. Lindsey had asked a prime question, the one I had yet to answer: "Why did this woman come to you in the first place?"

The door to Jared Malkin's house came open even as we were walking up the flagstones, past the carefully manicured desert plantings. Someone had told me these took as much water as the lawns and trees of the historic districts in Phoenix. Inside the doorframe stood a tall man with curly black hair, a shaggy black moustache, and a meaty face built around a pendulous red nose. His eyes fixed on Lindsey. I might as well have been one of the ocotillos whose blooms were dying in the summer heat.

But his voice and mannerisms seemed agitated even before we identified ourselves.

"You must have the wrong house," he said.

"You're Jared Malkin?" Lindsey asked.

"Yes, but…"

"So how could we have the wrong house?"

"All right, all right, come on inside," he said, and disappeared into the house. "No telling what the neighbors will think."

The great scholar Jacques Barzun celebrated a cultured person as one with a well-furnished mind. I didn't yet know about Malkin's mind, but the people that furnished motel rooms had decorated his house. It was all forgettable sofas, end tables, and desert scenes framed behind glass; maybe they were even bolted to the wall to keep guests from carting them away. There were no books. He led us back to a kitchen table and sat down. I went through it again, as I had with Shelley Baker. Malkin used a butter knife to put sardines slathered in mustard on a cracker. When he ate, his moustache became a broom for crumbs and yellow residue.

"So why do I care?" he said simply. He was continuously shaking his right leg.

"You're the managing partner of Arizona Dreams, right?"

"Right." He kept chomping and shaking his leg, both at about the same rhythm.

"Why would one of your top executives have her card found on the scene of a homicide?"

"Deputy, I don't have the foggiest goddamned idea. Are we done now?"

"No," I said. Then I went through the questions about Harry and Louie Bell, about the property west of Tonopah, about the school bus near Hyder. Did he know them? Had he been there? He kept shaking his head.

"Earl Rice?"

"Rice," he said. "Sure. He was a consulting hydrologist for Arizona Dreams."

"Who did what?" Lindsey asked.

"I don't have time to give lessons in development," he snapped. Then he smiled, "Even for a young lady with such beautiful dark hair and fair skin." You could almost smell cheap cologne coming off him. He went on, "The Groundwater Act of 1986—you gotta have a one-hundred-year supply of water, guaranteed, if you're going to do a project out in the desert, like Arizona Dreams. A consulting hydrologist is part of the process, so you can document the water supply for the state."

"A water supply anywhere?" Lindsey asked.

"No, no. It's got to be water on the property, under the ground, the aquifer."

"Have you heard from Mr. Rice lately?" I asked.

"No," Malkin said. "He retired about a year ago. I heard he moved down to Panama. Talk about getting a lot of house for the money. It's a steal in Central America. Lot of folks here are retiring down there."

I didn't mention Dana Earley. No need to tip our hand yet. I let things fall into silence. Let him fill it. Only the refrigerator motor whirred in the background. More sardine carcasses disappeared in Malkin's fast-moving maw. He had large dark pores on top of his cheekbones.

"Ha!" he said.

Ha, what? I glanced at Lindsey and waited.

"I knew you recognized me," he said to me. "It's true. I used to be Jerry von Shaft. That was my stage name."

I had no idea what he was talking about.

Lindsey asked what he was talking about.

"You're too young to remember, Miss," he said to Lindsey. "But those were great days. In 1978, I was one of the top-paid actors in adult films. Almost up there with John Holmes and Harry Rheems. You can still find me in DVD, films like *Revenge of the Horny Cheerleaders*. I play a detective, just like you guys. See, there was plot and acting. Great days, before I got too old and video rentals ruined the old adult entertainment business. Great way to pick up women, too. At least it used to be. After paying out for three marriages I can't even afford to get an erection in this town." He leered at Lindsey. "No offense, ma'am."

He ran an index finger around the empty sardine tin and then sucked the juice. "What was your favorite movie that I did?"

I shrugged my shoulders. I could name all the presidents, but here I was at a loss.

"Don't be shy." A wide smile expanded the bushy mustache. "Your pretty partner here won't tell your wife. Don't expect us to believe you spent the seventies in some library studying."

Lindsey said, "So you ended up in real estate in Phoenix?"

"Life's funny," he said. "Phoenix is a hick town. But it's sunny almost every day. I can play golf anytime I want. I get to live out here with the gazillionaires, and I'm paying about the same as I would for a shack in L.A. Guy can come over here, throw up a few houses, make a killing. You ought to try it."

"Why all the LLCs?" Lindsey asked.

Malkin smiled at her and shook his head.

"Arizona Dreams LLC also does business as AZD2 LLC, Sierra Montana LLC, and Camino Vista LLC. The land for your development changed hands with about two dozen limited liability corporations, by my count. And you secured a loan from Tonopah Trinity LLC. A lot of these LLCs have the same address."

He blinked several times, showing long lashes.

"You're very bright," he said, "and very beautiful."

"About the real killing," I said. "What about your trip to Malibu?"

His nostrils flared. "How the hell did you…? That goddamned Shelley loudmouth bitch. I was on a business trip. To meet one of my investors. I've been patient with you two until now, but you're starting to piss me off. Do you have any idea of the powerful people I have as partners in Arizona Dreams?"

"Ms. Baker made sure not to tell us," Lindsey said in her calm alto.

He looked at her a while, then smacked his lips and stood. I tried not to imagine him as Jerry von Shaft. He said, "Look, I wish I could help you. But I can't and I'm really in a hurry.

Something's come up. Always a bad day in the development business."

We walked toward the door, back through the anonymous living room to the anonymous foyer.

"I read somewhere that you destroyed Hohokam ruins," I said. This came from Lindsey's research on Malkin.

"Those weren't protected," he snapped. "I made sure. My lawyers checked and double-checked everything. I paid good money for that land. Do you have any idea how much it would have cost to bring in a bunch of archeologists, that kind of shit? The project wouldn't have been doable. And for what? A bunch of old mud walls, some pieces of pots? Give me a break."

"No value to history, huh?" I asked.

"You want history, Deputy," he said, "visit a fucking museum. Now, I really gotta go."

# Chapter Thirty-Two

In Maricopa County, a suspect's first hearing is called, logically, the initial appearance, or IA. Robin's came a little after eleven on Wednesday morning, in a small, sterile courtroom downtown. Lindsey had been strangely detached from her sister's fate, or perhaps still numb from the arrest the night before. She had done nothing, hadn't even tried to visit Robin. But already I could sense Peralta's hidden hand: When Robin was brought in wearing an orange jumpsuit, a tall, classically handsome man in a blue pinstripe suit announced he was representing her. This was James H. Goldstein, one of the top defense lawyers in town and one of Peralta's close friends and political supporters. Robin looked haggard and pale, her healthy tan seemingly confiscated at booking. I felt strange, being at an IA for a family member, and I saw Lindsey suppress a shiver.

But an hour later Robin was free, back in her civilian clothes and sitting in the back seat of the Prelude, headed home. Goldstein had made a meal of the assistant county attorney, who looked about 12 years old and was ill-prepared. The judge denied the state's request to hold Robin as a material witness and ordered her released, provided she stayed in the custody of her sister, the deputy sheriff. Kate Vare looked back at me from the prosecutor's table, and it wasn't a friendly look. Even though Robin was out of jail, I knew Vare would set aside her entire caseload to prepare a murder rap against Robin.

One of the first lessons I learned as a patrol deputy was that family fights are among the most lethal situations for the cops. Killing was more likely when the family members were cops. So I let the silent chill hang in the car. Neither Lindsey nor Robin spoke. I had never been with Robin where she was silent for so long. After a while, a fight, provided some catharsis came at the end, would have come as a relief. The only fight was one we saw at the Circle K gas pumps on McDowell and Seventh Avenue, two middle-aged women going at each other with fists in the gas line. Maybe they were sisters, too. Lindsey called 911.

"I want to see this property," Lindsey finally said, to me. "Let's drive out into the desert."

We stopped at Cypress Street to change clothes and load drinking water, then we drove back down Fifth Avenue to the Papago Freeway. In addition to a fuel shortage and gas lines, Phoenix had earned a smog alert that morning. The air was so dirty we couldn't even make out the White Tank or Estrella mountains until we were miles west of downtown. Even then, the scene couldn't have been more different from my memory of the clear, wild mountain range that day in February when I had gone to check out the body report given to me by Dana Earley. Now the White Tanks were reduced to a fuzzy brown apparition squatting against the dirty horizon. But it didn't seem to deter the homebuyers. Acres of rooftops had been added since I had last driven out this far. More "available" signs peppered the landscape. Fewer farm fields survived. After the Buckeye exits the subdivisions fell away and we were enveloped by the desert in high summer. Without our technological amulets of air-conditioned car and cell phones, we would have been frighteningly vulnerable.

Quitting Tonopah, I again took the exit at 335th Avenue. It still wasn't much of an avenue, and soon we were traveling over a graded dirt road. We rolled over the basin of the Harquahala Desert, surrounded by scrub and low cactus, and, at a distance, mountains. We were insignificant actors in this arena bounded by eternal spectators. Every mountain told its own fantastic story. I was no geologist, so I let my imagination play on the paintbrush strokes of light and dark, purple, dun, black, and gray. I watched the whorls, slopes, uplifts and ledges, the spectacular leaps and fortress walls. Other mountains were plain, giant dirt hills and subtle, brooding slopes covered with scrub. Ages and ages: God's canvas unprofaned by subdivisions and man. Against it we moved, just three people, at the dawn of the twenty-first century, trying to solve a murder. At least I hoped we all three shared that goal.

The Bell property looked much the same. Suddenly the desert was lush again, with towering saguaros, demonstrative ocotillos, standoffish yucca, barrel cactuses fat and content, and my old nemesis the cholla. Thick palo verdes marked the wash that was hidden in the deep cut just outside our view to the east. To the north, the land lifted in a steady slope from the road, headed toward the fez-shaped butte and the sharp-featured mountains beyond. When we all stepped out of the car and closed the doors it was as silent as deep space. But here the star of the solar system was close, and the heat threatened to overwhelm every other sense. Lindsey put on a floppy hat. Robin and I settled for sunglasses. I walked them up to the old gate, then down the rutted path to Harry Bell's cairn, explaining again what had happened that first day. The rocks had been neatly replaced over the grave, and as we got closer I noticed something else. A headstone, made of a shape and rock to fit in with its surroundings, stood at the western end of the cairn. *Harry Truman Bell,* was carved there, along with his years of birth and death. Then the words: *He loved this land.*

"Where did that come from?" Robin spoke for the first time.

"I don't know," I said. "Unless Louie paid for it before he died."

"Why did Dana want to bring you out here?" Lindsey asked softly, more to herself. "There's nothing here. It's miles from anywhere. Why did she want you to come out here, where two guys would attack you?"

"Could she have known that?" I said.

"I don't know," Lindsey said.

"They were supposed to be guarding another property, where they grazed cattle in the spring and some contractor had been doing illegal dumping."

"I know that's the story," Lindsey said. "It just seems too convenient, getting you out here, beating you. Maybe they meant to do more than that."

"Look at that depression in the ground over there," Robin said, pointing to an indentation in the slope. "That's a sinkhole. It might mean there's a cave. I did some caving with an old boyfriend…"

Lindsey turned away with an angry swing of her waist, and I knew what she was thinking. What could you believe about Robin?

Just then we heard a high distant roar, and two black diamonds darted through a canyon that cut its way between the northern mountain range. They were trailing brown exhaust: fighter jets from Luke Air Force Base. Then they banked, climbed, and shot across the desert heading south. The Barry Goldwater Gunnery Range was that direction. Before silence settled on the desert, I noticed that Lindsey had left us. She was walking up the slope toward the butte.

Robin touched my arm.

"David, please don't hate me."

"I don't hate you," I said. "I don't trust you."

"You felt something for me that night, David, I know you did." Her face was insistent under a sheen of perspiration.

"I didn't feel anything," I said. "Speaking of fakes, your boyfriend Edward was one, right?"

She stared at the ground. "I couldn't tell you I'd been seeing Alan. Lindsey would have freaked. 'Glad to see you after all these years, Sis, and by the way the corpse you just found was my boyfriend.' Alan had been after me to move in with him. Guess it's a good thing I didn't."

"And the black eye you had the night you showed up on our doorstep?"

"A little stage makeup I got at Bert Easley's." She took my hand, but I pulled away. "Oh, David. I had to have a story. I was scared. Can you believe me?"

"How the hell should I know?" My stomach was tied in the kind of knot that would baffle an Eagle Scout. "I just hope you're not a murderer."

"I didn't kill Alan," she said matter-of-factly. "But I know somebody was trying to hurt him."

"What are you talking about?"

"A couple of weeks before he was killed, Alan started getting phone calls in the middle of the night. He'd get out of bed and go in the other room and talk. At first I was really pissed, because I thought he was juggling me with his other girlfriends. The second time it happened, I went to the bedroom door and listened. Alan kept telling somebody no, and how what they were asking was impossible, he wouldn't do it. 'Quit threatening me.' I heard him say that at least twice, and then he said he would go to the police if this person didn't leave him alone."

"Did you ask him about it?"

"No," she said. She turned away from the sun, which was now far in the western sky. I moved to face her.

"That night," Robin said. "We went to First Friday, dinner at Cheuvront's, toured some of the galleries. But we'd been fighting all night."

"What about?"

"Why? I can't even remember."

"You'd better because the police and the prosecutor will want to know. Fighting can be a motive."

"I didn't!" she shouted, then pulled her voice down. "I didn't kill him. But when we were leaving Paisley Violin, this big pickup truck stopped by the sidewalk and the guy inside called Alan by name. So Alan walked over and talked to him. I couldn't hear, but it obviously upset Alan. I didn't even go home with him that night. I crashed with a girlfriend."

"What did the man in the truck look like?" I asked, feeling as if someone with cold hands was brushing against my neck.

"He was big, a white guy, shaved head," she said. "He had an amazing tat on his arm."

We turned to watch Lindsey returning from the slope of the butte.

"Look at this, all these plants," she said. "You walk up there and look in the distance and it doesn't look this way. There's a distinct change when you get within maybe three-quarters of a mile of this land." My wife was a gardener. She noticed things. She planted white flowers and oleanders so the blossoms would be the last things you saw in the twilight. But my darling was also a cop. She went on: "It came to me: this isn't about some pickpocket at a casino, or protection money for a check-cashing outlet, or Dana being blackmailed. It's not about any of that. Everything in this case started here, with this patch of desert. Now I know why somebody murdered to try to get this land."

I am so proud of my brilliant wife, and I should have let her go on. But suddenly the scales fell from my eyes, too, and I blurted it out: "There's an aquifer."

Robin said, "Holy fucking shit."

# Chapter Thirty-Three

The next day I ran down Jack Fife, the security consultant who had hired the two goons that welcomed me to the Bell property back in February. It was an overdue visit. With a little badge persuasion, his secretary told me where I would find him. It was one hundred ten outside, and I was on my own. Lindsey was baby-sitting Robin—"the prisoner" as she called her behind her back—at the house, using the Internet to work on our case. Lindsey said she didn't want to talk to Robin, because she would no doubt be called to testify against her. Instead, she spent hours going through real estate, tax, and court records related to Arizona Dreams and Jared Malkin. "He may act like a dumb-ass," she said. "But he's not dumb. Not with this complicated a paper trail."

So she had already armed me for my meeting with Jack Fife. I was on my own with Peralta. My reflexes wanted to report to him, especially tell him our hunch about the underground water on the Bell property. But it wasn't time yet. We didn't have it tied up. And if I caught him in the wrong mood, he might just shut us down and send the case to Pima County. Don't even send him an e-mail, Lindsey said: It could become public record if the case blew up into a political scandal.

I had little of the Machiavellian in me. I was onto something more elemental. Instead of intriguing as advised by *The Prince*, I was following one of the oldest dictates of the West: "Whiskey's for drinking, and water's for fighting over." Maybe, killing over. The sense grew in me each time I drove over a bridge that spanned one of the canals that are like the exposed arteries of Phoenix's lifeblood. This utterly unnatural city was the product of many water fights: whites against Indians, Arizona vs. California, Lower Basin battling Upper Basin, and everyone against the desert. Growth and prosperity in the West came with water. And far from the myth of rugged individualism, the water often came thanks to grand federal projects. Without them, Phoenix would have been nothing but a village. Donald Worster wrote about this ably in his book *Rivers of Empire*. I was only a little envious. And yet, history indicated the desert was a tenacious adversary if you chose to fight it. For proof, you only needed to recall the vanished civilization of the Hohokam, who built the first canals. Or the dropping water table in Pinal County. The desert repaid.

The noon rush was already thinning out when I arrived at La Perla. It was one of the oldest restaurants in town, wedged into a little block of downtown Glendale on the other side of the Santa Fe railroad tracks. Jack Fife was a squat man with a comb-over and wearing a short-sleeved dress shirt and a wide blue tie. He didn't seem surprised when I slid into the booth across from him.

"My name's David…"

"I know who you are, Mapstone," he said. "Chips?" He pushed a basket toward me and went back to a giant plate of cheese enchiladas. "You're Peralta's history boy."

"You provide security people for the real estate business," I said.

"Sure," he said. "That's part of what I do. Developers and property owners hire me. You know, keep away the tree huggers, the environmental terrorists, the thieves." He chewed and talked, a string of cheese suspended from his lower lip. "How 'bout those gas lines, huh? I hear some guy shot a gas station attendant in Mesa last night. Doesn't take much to turn people to animals, especially in this hick town. When I came here from LA thirty years ago it was a hick town, and it's still a hick town."

"Why do you stay?"

"I'm here for the lifestyle," he said, dabbing hot sauce on his food like an inattentive priest sprinkling holy water.

"Last February, your boys got a little zealous with me, out west of Tonopah."

"Look," he said, wiping his mouth, then his forehead, with a napkin. "I cleared all that up. They were protecting another property. It was all a mistake. I fired the assholes, and you guys put them in jail for assault."

He wadded up the napkin and put it on the table. "Why are you bothering my lunch, Mapstone? I already got that reflux thing. Wakes me up in the middle of the night with this acid coming out of my throat. Getting old sucks."

His entire face seemed to press in on itself from top and bottom as he gave a grimace of pain.

"Getting old sucks," I agreed. I watched him, played a hunch. I made no claim to being a great detective. Kate Vare didn't think I was a real cop at all. I was just the history shamus, taking a leave from writing Peralta's book. I would have been happier researching a crime from 1920. But this case had acquired its own internal propulsion. Too many people had died already. And Lindsey and I were stuck in the middle of it. I tightened my abdomen, as if expecting a punch. In a business voice, I said, "You have the right to remain silent."

"Wha…?"

"You have the right to remain silent. Anything you say can be used against you."

He laughed and coughed. "What the fuck are you Mirandizing me for? Have some chips…"

"You have the right to an attorney…"

"Oh, you're a hard ass cop, huh? You don't do it well."

"You have the right to an attorney."

"Yeah, yeah," he said, giving a dismissive wave of his napkin, "and if I can't afford one, the county will appoint one for me. Quit dicking with me. I was on the Mesa force for twenty years. I think I know the bit. Why the hell you trying to come after me now, for something that happened six months ago and has all been settled." He scooped a huge piece of enchilada in his mouth. Through bites he said, "My lawyer's gonna love this false arrest case."

"Your guys weren't protecting the other property," I said. "I talked to the landowner this morning. He didn't know anything about it. He's never heard of you."

Fife put his fork down and picked out a pack of Camels. He lit one. His hand shook.

"So," I said, "the sheriff would naturally wonder why your employees were out there. When they attacked me, they were nowhere near the other land anyway. They were on the Bell property."

"So maybe Bell hired us to do that?" Fife muttered.

"Why didn't you say that in the first place," I said.

"Well…"

"Why didn't Louie Bell tell that to the deputies when they were talking to him?" I said. "He said he didn't know anything about them."

"I do a lot of security," Fife said. "I don't even remember the particulars of that. Look, it was a couple of bad apples…"

"It was almost as if they were out there looking for trouble," I said. "I didn't see any environmental terrorists out there, Jack. There wasn't anything to steal, either. It was like they were looking to teach somebody a lesson."

"Look, Mapstone…"

He stared at me, little eyes imploring. I went on, "We know that Tom and Dana Earley were trying to buy that thousand acres from Louie Bell, and Louie was balking."

"I don't know anything about this," he said. "Tom Earley, the county supervisor?"

"Tom Earley was sending letters demanding that the sale go through. Somebody else was doing more than writing letters. A little muscle to encourage the old coot. Then he ends up dead, in a casino, with an ice pick in his ear."

"What're you telling me this for?" he said, rolling his head around his fat neck, taking a drag on the Camel.

"You sent muscle out to the property, Jack. I met them."

"The Earleys are good, God-fearing people," he pleaded. He was sweating profusely now, matting down his comb-over and soiling his short-sleeved shirt.

I just sat and watched him. Then, "Maybe you had Louie Bell killed. There was a lawyer working with the Earleys named Alan Cordesman. He was killed with an ice pick, too. Pretty high body count for a land deal, Jack."

"I don't know any Cordesman." He suppressed a violent belch and made a face. He stubbed out what was left of the Camel and lit another, sucking on it greedily.

"You like to hire out muscle, Jack," I went on. "I've had a run-in with a big man who has a tattoo that covers his entire upper arm. The same man was seen at Louie Bell's trailer, and trailing Cordesman. Does he work for you?"

"No!"

"What about blackmail, Jack. Did Dana Earley hire you because she said she was being blackmailed?"

"She never said anything!" He pounded the table. "I don't know what you're talking about."

He stared at me. He had small dark reptilian eyes. The effect was completed with his tongue darting in and out after each puff on the cigarette. He said, "You don't know anything. You're bluffing."

A bus girl came and took away the plate of food. Fife had barely touched it. I said, "We have documents."

"You...you can't."

"We have the documents," I repeated. "Now we also know that after Louie Bell died, somebody came in and paid the taxes on the property and bought it. The new owner is called Tonopah Trinity LLC."

"This is all too complicated," he said.

"It's pretty simple, Jack. Two old desert rats who didn't want to sell their land. One of them was so cantankerous he had himself buried out there. The other wouldn't accept any price for the land. Imagine that, in Arizona. But somebody wouldn't take no for an answer. So when Louie Bell is killed, and it looks at first like it was the work of some street punk, the bureaucratic wheels turn and the county gets its back taxes, and the Bell property is finally sold. Winners and losers. The quick and the dead. It's pretty simple."

"So, ask this Trinity whatever," he said weakly. "Ask 'em."

"The agent who's on the registration form is just some guy sitting in an office in Chandler, and he doesn't know anything. I'm learning that's how a lot of business is done around here. We've got to protect the privacy of these swells. But I bet you can tell me who really owns Tonopah Trinity."

He stared out into the empty restaurant and blew a long plume of smoke in the direction of the front window.

I said, "Tonopah Trinity LLC."

Fife stabbed out the cigarette, instantly picked out another and lit it. He was fighting hiccups. A bright mariachi tune belted out of the jukebox, but I could hear his voice.

"I'll be damned if I'm going down for Tom Earley," he said.

# Chapter Thirty-Four

By three o'clock I was back downtown, and for the first time in days I was sitting alone in my office on the fourth floor of the old county courthouse. The lock had been replaced, but the room was still musty with my suspicions. It wouldn't have surprised me if Kate Vare had broken in. But, no, that wasn't her style. So who? The tattooed man? Dana Earley, perhaps? She certainly knew where my office was located. So much had happened since the break-in that it seemed like ancient history. Aside from the low growl of traffic outside, the room was still. My Hollinger boxes and folders of research for the book looked foreign and unkempt. Somewhere, real historians were working. Just a few years ago, one found a trove of letters written by St. Augustine, launching a hundred academic conferences and a shelf of new books.

Me? In my desk, I had a fake letter confessing to a murder that never happened. *Washington's Crossing* was still on the desk top. I started reading it for distraction, but my mind heard the ghosts of the old jail on the top floor. I put on my headphones, put a Sinatra CD in the player, and put my feet on the desk. I imagined Lindsey as a teenage mother, Robin succumbing to drugs and the street, and their lives of chaos. Sinatra's lonely message was the perfect mixer, and my throat caught. So much loss.

The door swung open violently and slammed into the door-stop. It was a wonder the pebbled glass in the door didn't shatter—and I knew it would take months if ever for the county to pay for its replacement. Standing before me was a short man with news anchor hair, a blue suit and red tie. He was sweating like a leaky pipe. His face was dyed with the scarlet of embarrassment or rage. But I didn't think he was embarrassed. His name was County Supervisor Tom Earley. I removed the headphones.

"You little son of a bitch!" he yelled and stormed toward the desk. I was never good in workplace confrontations, which can be especially vicious in universities. So I just stood up and watched him as he advanced stiff-legged across the room. For a "little son of a bitch," I was more than a head taller than my accuser.

"You're done here!" he said, slamming his fist on the old desk. One of the Hollinger boxes tipped over, depositing files on the wood floor. "Pack up your things…no, don't you touch anything! You are to give me your badge and gun, and leave this building immediately."

Later, I would imagine the fun from pulling out the Colt Python—in response to his command, of course—just to see his expression. I just stood my ground and glanced at the 1905 photo of Carl Hayden, when he was Maricopa County Sheriff. He'd know how to deal with the likes of Earley. I tried to mimic Hayden's straight-lipped stoicism. Only a few layers of my stomach wall were burned off by stress.

"Now!" he shrieked, sticking a stubby finger in my face. I didn't see what Dana saw in him, or rather I did, and better understood her desire to play with Jerry von Shaft, er, Jared Malkin.

I sat down and said, "I'll leave when the sheriff tells me."

"You little son of a bitch," he said. "How dare you snoop and spy on me."

There was nothing to say yet, so I just sat in silence. Working as partner for the Sphinx-like Peralta has taught me to even enjoy silence. After only a few seconds, Earley resumed his tirade. "Arizona Dreams is the most important development in this state's history. I did nothing wrong as an investor. There was no significant county vote where I had a conflict of interest." I made note of that interesting locution. He ranted on: "Do you have any idea of who you are dealing with? Not just me. Some of the most powerful men in the state!"

"Was it a good deal for you?" I asked.

"You stay out of my life! Out of my family's life!" He was so short that we were about eye-level when he was standing and I was sitting. He seemed taller in television headshots.

"I'm not going to fire you!" he said suddenly. "I've just decided that…"

"Gee, I thought there were five county supervisors, and all this time I was wrong. There's only you." What the hell. If I was a goner, may as well go out in style.

"Shut up!" he shouted. "I'm going to ruin you. You'll never even teach Mexican kids in some public school, much less be a professor again, when I'm done with you. You'll never work in law enforcement. I know your kind. Liberals. Professors. The filth you teach our kids…"

"I was considered a fascist at the faculty club," I said.

"You are! A fascist socialist communist atheist liberal, just like all your kind." Tom Earley's discount political science theory. He theorized on: "You're the kind that probably disapproves of Arizona Dreams. You want to save the desert." This in a sing-songy voice. "Look, this is private property. We'll never let you liberals take away private property rights. Why, this is America!"

"What are you talking about?"

He looked at me oddly, as if I had snapped him out of something. Then the rage returned to his eyes. "I'll ruin you, Mapstone. I'll bring you up at every supervisors meeting. I'll find out what you're really doing here. I'll get that wife of yours…"

"Leave Lindsey out of this, or we're not going to be so friendly." I said it in a normal voice, but he stepped back.

"I'll use you to ruin Peralta," he hissed. "We'll see what your tune is then."

I picked up *Washington's Crossing* and opened the book. I did it to piss him off. I could almost hear his internal boiler start to go critical. "It's a good book," I said. Then: "Why did your wife come to see me last February, Supervisor?"

"She didn't. What the hell are you talking about?"

"She claimed she had been one of my students at Miami University."

"You're insane. She attended Mesa Community College. She's never even been to Florida."

"Ohio."

"She's never been!" He was shouting again. It made me glad my end of the building was deserted except for my office.

"First Dana said she had discovered a letter from her late father, and he was admitting to murdering a man and burying him out in the desert. Then Dana claimed she was being blackmailed, and she was trying to protect you."

"Her father is still alive," he said, in a softer, hoarse voice. He was watching me closely.

"That makes sense," I said. "Because that desert land belonged to a pair of brothers named Bell. One of them was buried out there. We wasted a lot of taxpayer money clearing that one up. But it was a chance to see some pretty desert at least. Valuable, too, I'd guess."

Earley had drifted back toward the big windows facing First Avenue. His color had gone from scarlet to ashen even before I said, "I'm sure you know about that property, Supervisor."

Earley started to walk toward me when there was a blur in the hallway, and then we weren't alone anymore. The tall man with the shaved head was wearing a long-sleeved work shirt, and then I realized why he might want to conceal his prized tattoo: to make an easy escape, with no identifying characteristic. Funny the trivia your mind cooks up when facing oblivion. He had a black pistol in his hand. It looked like what you'd get if you mated a semiautomatic pistol with a machine gun, producing an unwieldy long magazine and a thick barrel with holes like Swiss cheese. In other words, it was a Tek-9, and it could easily be converted from semi- to fully automatic.

"No sap this time?" I asked.

"Don't even think about it," he said, indicating the Python on my belt. The nasty-looking Tek-9 was in a clean line with my heart, which was now thumping like a washing machine on imbalance. "Pull it out slow, with your left hand, and put it on the desk, with the butt facing me."

He'd obviously done this before. Right then I had a lot of wishes. I wished I were in my wife's arms in a safe place where it rained. I wished I wasn't sitting down, and that the damned history book was not still in my right hand. I said, "I'm not giving up my weapon. Be a bad habit to get into." I didn't recognize my own voice, but my body obeyed the first rule of Peralta's training.

The thick barrel came up toward my face. I think the tattooed man would have killed me right then, but Earley spoke and said, "Adam, what are you doing?"

The man he called Adam said simply, "You" and turned the pistol toward Earley's head. Earley let out a whimpered "Wait!" but it was enough time for me to fling *Washington's Crossing* at Adam. I hit him right between the eyes and his head and shoulders lurched back like a puppet whose limbs were attached to rubber bands. Instantly there was a sharp explosion from the Tek-9, but I was diving under the desk and drawing out the Python. When I came up, Tom Earley was still standing, his swoosh of hair in place, and Adam was already halfway to the stairway atrium.

# Chapter Thirty-Five

By the time I got out the front door of the old courthouse, the tattooed man was halfway to Washington Street. He turned and pointed the thick barrel, which had its desired effect: I dived to the ground behind one of the columns. The heated sidewalk burned my hands. You never can find a cop when you need one. There were probably more police officers, deputies, and U.S. marshals in the few blocks surrounding me than anyplace in the entire Southwest. But I saw no uniforms on the street; heard no commands to stop. I lifted myself off the concrete and raced down the steps. He ran into the one-way street, provoking screeching tires and honking horns. Somebody rear-ended a taxi. The horns stopped abruptly when they saw the hardware he was carrying. Then he was on the north side of the street, by the front entry to the Wells Fargo Tower. But no bankers appeared. It was so hot that the sidewalk was deserted. I cut through the desert plantings and shadows in front of the courthouse. He was jogging east, concealing the gun inside his shirt, and momentarily not checking his rear. I saw a chance.

I holstered the Python for better running and sprinted diagonally across the intersection with First Avenue, somehow avoiding a mail truck that didn't see me. Then I was pumping my arms, beating the pavement with my feet, coming up behind him fast. He didn't see me before I tackled him, ramming him hard into the railing at Tom's Tavern. We went over, crashing into tables and chairs. I landed on him, and saw the Tek-9 skitter across the floor toward the restaurant door. That triumph lasted all of a few seconds before a fist smashed into my nose. Somehow he had managed to wriggle and turn and get me at a disadvantage. But there was no analyzing going on at that moment. It was all shock and pain. I fell backward into a capsized table; that brought another jolt of pain. Somehow a reflex back in my brainstem had my hand reaching for the Python. But by the time I focused, he was gone.

"Call nine-one-one," I said, sounding very congested, when a restaurant employee stuck her head out the door. "Tell them a plainclothes deputy is pursuing an armed suspect." I got to my knees, then to my feet, and wobbled off up First Avenue. I was dizzy and my shirt was dappled with blood.

The sun went behind a skyscraper, but the heat was starting to beat me down. Now that the original adrenaline rush had worn off, I was conscious of being covered in sweat, my lungs were burning, my stomach bloated with heat nausea. It was probably only one hundred seven degrees out, magnified by the concrete. I tried to focus on the suspect, waited to hear sirens or see uniforms. Adam had been slowed down, too. I saw him a block ahead, crossing the street. His head snapped to the west: He was thinking about going into the Orpheum Lofts. Then he changed his mind, running and limping back across the street. Then we were going east on Adams Street. I'd like to say it was like Manhattan, and he couldn't see me behind him for all the crowds on the sidewalks. But this was Phoenix, and nobody was out here with us. The sun brutally re-emerged, glaring off the storefronts, cooking the street. He kept looking back at me, but for some reason didn't shoot. I stayed as close to the walls and alleyways as I could, so I could find cover quickly. Maybe he thought he could just outrun me.

Then he was gone.

A tectonic cramp cut through my middle. I leaned against the wall beside Quiznos and barfed on the sidewalk. The suave David Mapstone. I thought my guts were going to come out onto the concrete. I couldn't catch a breath. Everything was hot.

My sweat-soaked shirt hung on me. I felt out of shape. I felt old.
I looked around. Nothing. I cursed the sidewalk.

Then I saw movement across the street. It was the Central
Avenue entrance to the Wyndham Hotel. Maybe the door had
just finished swinging shut. It was worth a try. I did my best to
jog across at the light, ignoring a voice inside that said, "wait
for the cavalry."

Then I was in the darkened corridor of the hotel entrance.
The air conditioning collided with my superheated skin. The
heavy-duty hotel carpet felt like the greatest luxury my feet had
ever known. But the heavy weight of the Python reminded me
of the task at hand. I hastily hung my badge on my belt so some
trigger-happy rookie didn't take me out. I moved slowly toward
the front desk. It was quiet and I began worrying about the dark
potential of the man with the Tek-9 in downtown Phoenix.
I slowed my pace, looked toward the lobby, which looked as
deserted as the street outside. I knelt down ahead of where the
wall opened up into the larger space of the lobby. It was an
old trick, to look around a corner from a level where someone
wouldn't naturally notice. My knees hurt like hell.

"Sir, are you all right?" This came from a perky blonde behind
the counter. So much for my subterfuge. I asked if she were safe.
She said she was. Everything seemed normal. I stood up and
approached the desk.

"Oh, my God! Do you want me to call an ambulance!"

I must have looked quite a sight. "Did a man come through
here?" I asked. "Tall, wearing a work shirt?"

"He just came through," she said. "He went that way." She
indicated the east entrance. "Hey, are you okay?"

I was already running down the corridor. I wasn't okay. I
wasn't in my right mind, to be chasing a man armed with an
automatic weapon. But if I couldn't catch him, I might never
know why he was ready to kill County Supervisor Tom Earley.
I pushed open the glass doors, and was in the shade of the walkway. He was walking east on Monroe Street by the Chase Tower
garage. I willed my legs to move, and then I was crossing First

Street at a trot. Panels of sidewalk passed under my feet. Step on a crack, break your mother's back. Step on a crack, get shot.

"Deputy sheriff, stop! Stop!" I drew down on him with half a block between us, but I had faith in the Python's accuracy. With a little luck, the hollow point bullet wouldn't go through him and take out a civilian.

He had no such qualms. He raised the Tek-9 and nothing happened. Just then, a woman walked across Second Street, and I didn't fire. Adam screamed a profanity and ran, working the gun's action. Jammed. I ran toward him, keeping the Python in a combat grip. I caught up with him at Second Street. Only a crosswalk separated us. Finally, I heard sirens, a lot of them. But somebody else was on the corner, one of the downtown guides. Adam punched him in the middle and shoved him to the ground.

"Don't come any closer, Mapstone!" He knew my name. I crossed the street, keeping him in my sights.

"I'll kill him! I swear to God!" He aimed the jammed Tek-9 at the guide. The guide wore a shirt that said, "Ask Me!" Behind us, the statues of the Herberger Theater Center cavorted with the muses. The sun went behind the Hyatt Regency, extending shade across the street.

"Put your weapon down slowly," I commanded between panting breaths.

"Fuck you!" He was still fighting with the jammed action of the pistol. Suddenly a piece of metal made a sliding sound and a shell ejected out of the top. I fired from ten feet away.

# Chapter Thirty-Six

A dust storm was coming in Friday night when I stepped through the door into Portland's bar. I said hello to a few people I knew. They wanted to know if I was safe—the shooting had been on every television station and in the newspapers. I looked around the bar. Many people were dressed in artist black, giving me hope that Phoenix might become a real city. There wasn't time to linger. I was meeting someone. There she was, sitting at a table, wearing a blouse that was as orange as her hair. She smiled as I approached. I nodded at her and sat down.

"David," she said, "I can't imagine what you've been through. Are you all right? Are you hurt? Thank God. I know you're on leave, because of the shooting. That's got to be routine, right? If this wasn't justified…"

I let the bartender bring me a Beefeater martini. Before Dana sat a full glass of white wine.

"There's good news," she said. "The gas pipeline has been fixed. I won't have to drive forever to fill up that SUV." I said nothing, and in a moment she asked, "Do they know anything about who this man was?"

"His name was Adam Perez," I said. "Thirty years old. He had a record of assault and attempted murder."

"He was obviously the one who was blackmailing us," she said. "Even so, it can't feel good to kill a man."

I said it didn't feel good. I watched the ice crystals float across the top of the martini glass, then took a sip.

"David," she went on. "I'm actually glad you asked me to meet you tonight. I wanted to thank you, of course, for saving Tom's life. Maybe he won't be so down on you and the Sheriff's Office now."

"Maybe," I agreed.

"And I also wanted to explain myself a little better," she said.

I didn't say anything. She looked much the same way as the first time she came into my office. She had pretty green eyes, an average mouth, a weak chin. She still had butterscotch in her voice. Her hair fell to her shoulders in a respectable bob. It was the perfect voice and face for a liar. She saw me watching her and smiled at me. I watched the wind rustle the palm trees out on Central Avenue and raise dust from the light-rail construction.

"When I couldn't meet you at El Pedregal," she said, "I know what you must have thought. I wanted to. I wanted to show you the blackmail letters. But I told Tom what I was doing and he forbade me to go."

"You don't strike me as the kind who can be told no," I said.

She sipped her wine and pursed her lips. "We're a pretty traditional family," she said. "I had to do as he asked. He wouldn't even let me call you again."

"Maybe it's just as well," I said. "Adam Perez came into the gallery that night, and he wasn't browsing. I never knew if he was after you or me…"

"Oh!" Her mouth was a perfect lipstick doughnut. "Oh, I'm so sorry. Thank God that horrible man won't hurt anyone again. And you'll have to forgive me if I say the same about Mister Louis Bell, who put him up to all this to ruin my husband—and when that didn't work, to kill poor Tom."

"It's a happy ending."

She beamed and took my hands across the table. "Yes, thank you, Professor Mapstone."

I was watching a blonde getting teary at the next table, describing something to a friend: the boyfriend who won't commit, the workplace slight that she wouldn't remember in a year. Outside the window, a homeless man struggled by, his shirt standing out in the wind.

"Dana," I said, "you're still lying."

She let go of my hands and her smile blew off down Central.

"We have the documents," I said. "They make it clear that you and your husband were trying to buy the Bell property. They make it seem like a pretty desperate thing. Bell was resisting and you weren't taking no for an answer."

She gave a wounded cry. Several bar patrons looked over. She stared out the window.

"Before you tell the next set of lies, you should know that I've talked to Jack Fife, and he told me your husband hired a couple of men from him. He said your husband made it clear he wanted the men to put a scare into Louie Bell. Those are the same two men who assaulted me the day I went out there on your wild goose chase. He's signed a statement. He'll testify."

Dana's profile might as well have been cut out of marble. She didn't move. She watched the traffic snake through the construction on Central. A palm frond blew into the glass and smacked it. She didn't react. I just let her be. I had said my part. Finally, she crumpled over and sobbed. Her back heaved and shook through the orange blouse. I made no move to comfort her. When she looked back at me, her eyes were bloated and her fair complexion had turned bright pink.

"Look," she said, in a flat voice. "I took a vow to honor and obey…but…but…" She sighed and wiped away tears. "I just can't any more." She drained her glass in a single chug and signaled for another. She said, "I can't cover for Tom any more."

She pulled her chair close to me, so that we were almost knee-to-knee. "Now only the truth," she said.

"Dana," I said. "You know I still work for the sheriff's department. Anything you say to me could be incriminating. You don't have to tell me…"

She waved it away. "It's time. Long past time." She managed a smile. "And you wouldn't hurt me, David. You were my favorite professor, remember?"

"I don't," I said.

"You're a heart-breaker, David Mapstone," she said. "You were back then, too. Didn't even know I wanted to throw myself at you. And I was pretty then. I was thin."

A new glass arrived and she drank half of it. I stayed with one martini.

"We're deeply in debt," Dana said. "Tom was never a particularly good businessman. And he's a terrible gambler, but he's addicted. He can't stop himself. He has half a million dollars in gambling debts. So much for the values candidate." She gave a rueful laugh.

"When Tom had a chance to buy into Arizona Dreams, he was flat broke," she said. "So the partnership made him a loan. It was good to have his name associated with the project. It helped them get other influential investors. And Tom Earley was going to be governor someday—everybody said it. If we could just have held our own, having a stake in Arizona Dreams would have meant everything. A good education for Madison and Noah. A good retirement for us. But Tom couldn't stop gambling."

"He went to the casinos?" I asked.

"He was way beyond gambling here," she said. "And it would have been bad for his image. He went to high-stakes games out in north Scottsdale. They have orgies out there, too, you know. And he went to Vegas as Mister Thomas. So, anyway, at one of these games he meets this hydrologist named Earl Rice, and Earl told him about the Bell property. It's got water under the land, a lot of it. But it's not near anything, so it wasn't widely known that the water was there."

"Why?" I asked. "Why would Rice share his secret?"

"He was as in debt as Tom, but he didn't know Tom was in debt. Earl thought he was making a partner out of this big political leader who could help him. So they scraped together some money. They got another guy they met at the games, named Cordesman, who was a lawyer. They went in together to buy out the Bells. Only it didn't work out that way. Harry Bell hated the developers and he never wanted to see that land sold. When he died, he had himself buried out there. Louie Bell might have been open. But after Harry died, Louie said he'd made his brother a promise not to sell. It was insane. The partners were low-balling Bell, sure, but it would have been more money than he ever had. Tom just knew if he got that land it would be appealing as a resort, or a new town. He could flip it to somebody else for a fortune."

She blew her nose into a cocktail napkin. "It doesn't matter now," she said. "We lost our stake in Arizona Dreams today. The investors brought in a man from Malibu. Somebody with real money, one of those rich ones you've never heard of. Somebody named Dimah something-or-other. All the foreigners have the money now, you know. And they restructured the partnership, and Tom was out." She corrected herself. "We're out. All our hopes, hell."

I said, "So Tom hired the muscle?"

"I didn't know about it at the time," she said. "I swear, David. He just wanted to scare the old man."

"The old man ended up dead," I said.

Her shoulders heaved and she started crying again. "I know," she sobbed. "Once I would have said Tom couldn't possibly do anything like that. Now, I don't know. Are you married? Of course you are. How well do we know anyone, especially our husband or wife?"

"Did Adam Perez work for Fife?"

She shook her head. "He was another thing that crawled out from Tom's gambling life. Tom promised to make him a partner in the deal."

"So more than sadism was motivating him. Why would Adam try to kill your husband?"

"Tom was going to cut him out," she said.

"Why did you come to me?" I asked.

She laughed bitterly. "I had read about you in the papers, and I thought about just looking you up and seducing you. Fulfill my old college fantasy. But I tried to make the marriage work. Then Tom started taking shots at you and Sheriff Peralta. He kept talking about you, this hippie professor who was a bad influence in the Sheriff's Office. How ironic. He didn't know I knew you. He wanted me to come to you with a bogus historical case that would get you out to the Bell property. He wanted to provoke some kind of incident that would put pressure on Louie Bell. If you were beaten up on Bell's property…"

"And it could have been used by your husband to embarrass the sheriff."

She nodded slowly. "Then he came up with the blackmail story. It was a lie. But, my God, I never knew you would be in any danger…"

She took my hands. "David," she said. "I'm so sorry! I wanted to tell you the truth. That night, when I told you I had to meet you in Carefree, I was going to tell you everything. But Tom came home early. He started quizzing me, where was I going. I blurted something out. He told me he would kill me if I told anyone. David, I believed him."

She stared at me, eyes bright with tears.

"Please help me," she pleaded.

"OK," I said, reading her eyes.

And she leaned over and kissed me.

In a few minutes I paid the bill and I walked the soccer mom to her SUV. The wind was still gusting, but the dust had passed and the night was clear and hot and evocative. I walked back toward the door to Portland's, and to the old white Honda Prelude that was parked directly in front. I opened the door and slid into the passenger seat.

Lindsey smiled at me and poked me in the side. "You've really got to stop kissing strange women, Dave."

I tousled her bangs. "Did you get it?"

"Every word," she said, patting the DVD recorder sitting on the back seat. "And," she said, "I've finally met someone who lies more than my sister."

# Chapter Thirty-Seven

Dana's gray SUV pulled out of the parking garage and turned south on Central. Lindsey slipped the Prelude into drive and fell in about a block behind. Lightning shot across the eastern sky, but the wind had died down and the air only smelled vaguely of dust. The ballpark glowed under its closed roof. Thirty thousand Diamondbacks fans were inside, in the air conditioning, and until the game wound down the streets of downtown would be deserted except for a few pedicabs and cops. At Van Buren, Dana dutifully signaled, slowed, and turned right.

"This isn't the straight path back to the suburbs," Lindsey said. She followed, and we drove west through the northern edge of what city boosters hopefully called the Capitol Mall district, because of its proximity to the state capitol. Once it had held some of the loveliest houses in town, including most of Phoenix's small stock of Victorian homes. That was before the seventies and eighties, when abandonment and drug dealers had turned it into a war zone. Blocks of houses had been leveled. While other cities had been saving their painted ladies, Phoenix, so new, so much land, saw no reason. Now the area was slowly coming back, but nothing could replace the loss. On Van Buren, we passed a darkened car wash, the old bakery, a liquor store, a park fenced off as securely as a military installation, another liquor store. My old girlfriend Gretchen had an apartment near here, in a building that dated from territorial days.

Dana crossed Nineteenth Avenue and the railroad tracks, and the street became progressively poorer. The signs changed to mostly Spanish: La Raza Motors, Llanteria Hispania, Yerberia San Francisco. But people were out on the narrow sidewalks, and appearing as dark phantoms in front of car headlights as they jaywalked. This was definitely not Dana's part of town. After Twenty-Seventh Avenue she drove slower, and home boys in their low-slung custom Hondas buzzed around her. At Thirty-Fifth Avenue, she turned around in the parking lot of a Taco Bell. There were only five taquerias on every block in this part of Phoenix, and yet here was Taco Bell. Maybe the new migrants wanted to eat like real Americans, at a Taco Bell. On another night I would be telling all this to Lindsey. But my middle was tight with anxiety as Dana turned back onto Van Buren and headed east. Where the hell was she going? After a few blocks, she turned into an old drive-in.

"Jimmy Jacks?" Lindsey said.

"It was a hangout when I was a patrol deputy."

"I didn't even know they had cars back then, Dave."

"It was a horse drive-in. A gallop-in."

"This is very weird," Lindsey said, passing the drive-in, and turning into an alleyway. Indeed, here was Dana getting out in her suburban clothes from Kohl's and walking over to the window to order a Coke. Around her were immigrant men in their cowboy hats, and young Latinas in T-shirts and miniskirts. Dana's body language didn't look uncomfortable. Only five minutes passed when a cream-colored vintage Porsche coupe pulled into the lot and Dana got in. Jared Malkin was driving.

"Seems like a lot of trouble to meet your boyfriend," Lindsey said.

"Not if you're going to report what happened in your meeting with Mapstone," I said.

This time there was no leisure driving. Malkin gunned the Porsche east on Van Buren and Lindsey had to goose the Prelude to keep him in sight. He raced through the yellow light at Nineteenth Avenue veering north and Lindsey blew through the red as her tires screeched in protest at the tightness of the turn. He turned again on Roosevelt and Lindsey followed, letting space gather between the cars. In a few blocks, the little cream car did another of its sudden tacks.

"He's going into that alley," I said. Lindsey shut off her lights and pulled to the curb. We sat in silence on the otherwise deserted street. A few abandoned shopping carts sat nearby.

"You're pretty smart for a propeller-head."

"You'd better hope I'm right," she answered quietly.

I watched cars cross in the distance at Grand Avenue, and soon enough time passed that I began to worry. But then a creamy blur came back out of the alley with his lights off, came in our direction.

"Get down!"

We both tried to scrunch down around the console. Neither of us had the presence of mind to simply drop the seat back.

"This is pretty intimate," I said.

Lindsey said, "I always knew undercover work could be fun."

"I'll take you under cover."

That would have to wait. Lindsey swung the car around, also with headlights off, and followed at a distance. Back at Nineteenth Avenue, I saw the Porsche's taillights come on, and he turned south.

"Now we know he's afraid of being followed," Lindsey said. "And he knows some basics of evasive driving."

I said, "Or Dana does."

"You've got a thing for that soccer mom, Dave."

I said, "Ma Barker was a soccer mom, too."

By now, we'd returned to Van Buren and once again were heading west. The road was crowded enough that we could follow by a few car lengths and not be conspicuous. At Twenty-Seventh Avenue, the Porsche turned right. By the time we made the turn, it was gone.

"There," I said.

They had pulled into a driveway by a gate. Lindsey drove past. After a couple of blocks she wheeled around and parked so we could watch. The car sat at the entrance to a large terminal of some sort. It stretched for what looked like a quarter of a mile, a modern warehouse with numerous doors for trucks to load and unload cargo. But it was dark and abandoned-looking. Only the white of the walls glowed out at the street. We watched as Malkin unlocked a gate, swung it open and returned to the car. They then drove across the empty parking lot and stopped the car beside a loading dock. Again, Malkin got out and disappeared inside a door. In a few minutes, one of the large loading doors came up. This time Dana left the car and entered the warehouse.

"Are they hiding the car?" Lindsey asked.

I watched it for a minute and said, "Maybe they're using the headlights for illumination. Maybe the power's off…"

"Let's go over," Lindsey said.

"What?"

"Let's go," she said. "I'd say this is hot pursuit. You'd rather wait all night for a warrant?"

I thought I knew what she had in mind, and I wasn't so sure it was a good idea. We stepped out into the hot night and sprinted across Twenty-Seventh Avenue.

"You're obviously burning off a lot of frustration from being cooped behind a computer," I said, trying to keep up. We ran through the gate and made a dash for the side of the building. Out here we were exposed, but fortunately the vast parking lot was dark. Lindsey was wearing one of her customary black-top, black-jeans outfits, so she was mostly camouflaged, except for her fair skin. I did the best I could, wearing khakis and a black polo shirt. Once against the wall, we moved toward the open door. By this time, I was wearing what felt like an inch of sweat on the surface of my skin.

I caught Lindsey by the shoulder. "What are you going to say if they're standing just inside that door?" I whispered.

She shrugged and nodded toward the open cavern of the warehouse. "Ninety percent of successful police work is luck."

I pulled out my revolver and followed her. We stepped through the wide loading door, avoiding the track of the car headlights. It was instantly hotter, if that were possible, and smelled of dust and mold. Once my eyes adjusted, I could make out Dana and Malkin, illuminated across the concrete floor. They were standing maybe fifty feet away, amid a dense stand of loading pallets and other warehouse castoffs. One of them had a flashlight. They didn't know we were here. I could hear them talking, arguing. But I couldn't make out the words. Lindsey took my hand and pulled me into an alcove of the vast space, where we waited.

Little noises intruded from the street. Worries intruded in the dark: What if they were meeting people here, people who wouldn't appreciate finding us and might have the firepower to prevail in an argument? Enough time passed for me to consider leaning back against the wall, and think better of it. You never knew when you might encounter a black widow in a mood. Then something clicked in my head, and I knew why they had come here. Suddenly the voices were closer, coming toward us.

"It's there, goddammit." This was the voice of the demure soccer mom.

"We can't leave it here."

"Where else are we going to put it, Jared? In your trunk? You're such a dumb bastard sometimes."

"Don't be such a bitch, Dana," Malkin said. "I wanted to make sure. I don't trust things right now. This deputy is asking too many questions."

"He believes me," Dana said. "He likes me."

Lindsey poked me in the ribs.

"We can't just leave it here," Malkin said.

"Why not? You said this place might be vacant for years. Don't panic, Jerry…"

And then they were gone. I heard the door drawn down, the lights went out, and we were alone in the dusty void. Then Lindsey's pants leg became illuminated. She had brought a small black Maglite. She played the light around the big space. You could have played several football games in it simultaneously. Instead of echoing, the warehouse seemed to swallow sound. We walked toward the pallets.

"I wonder how long before we drop dead in here of heat exhaustion," I said.

"Dave, people pay good money for hot weather," she said. "Check it out, History Shamus."

She illuminated a cylindrical container, about the size of an oil drum. It was once maybe olive green, and had the markings of civil defense from the 1960s. But I doubted that it held drinking water as its lettering said.

"Wait back here." I took the flashlight and approached it. The "it" that was hidden, that should be moved, or might not be found for years. My stomach was tight and jumpy.

"What do you think, Dave?"

I knelt down and used the butt of the Maglite to push against the lip of the barrel. The walls of the barrel were surprisingly cool. Then I rested the flashlight against the metallic edge and tapped the other end with the heel of my hand. Again. Again. Then the top came ajar. The odor was instant and recognizable, primal and indescribable. Put it in a perfume bottle and call it Mortality. I coughed and fought my gag reflex and pried the lid all the way off.

"Dave?"

"Stay over there," I said, my throat constricted.

She protested but didn't come closer. "I'm not a baby...Oh, God, is that smell what I think it is?"

# Chapter Thirty-Eight

I got to my feet and walked back to Lindsey. She took my hand. "All right?" she asked. I nodded my head. I said, "Let's go outside and call the sheriff." My tongue tasted vile. My thirst was consuming—I was thirsty enough to kill for water. We crossed the huge room walking in our safe small cone of light, for otherwise everything else was black. It was impossible to sense space, whether the ceiling was three stories above us, or three miles, and the far wall was only a destination we held as a belief in the undiscovered country. For just a few moments I had lost the composure that had always been my gift in tight situations. If Lindsey had not been beside me, I think I might have gone mad with fear and rage. The world was dark. My thoughts were dark. "Death solves all problems," Joseph Stalin said. "No man, no problem." Somebody had been doing a hell of a lot of problem-solving for a piece of desert real estate in Arizona, even if it did have an aquifer under it. The hundred or so steps we took before we could make out the wall were not enough time to provide answers, or even the right questions.

And we weren't alone.

"That's far enough." The voice was Jared Malkin's and suddenly an intense light was in our face. I directed the small Maglite at him but it was no competition.

"Get your hands where I can see them!" he barked. I kept my right hand at my side, holding the Maglite with my left. There was no way to see if he was armed. Where the hell did he come from? Out of the corner of my eye, I could see that Lindsey had retrieved her baby Glock and was holding it at her side, partly concealing it inside her fingers and palm.

"Don't fuck with me, Mapstone!" Malkin shouted. "I've got a gun and I will use it!" To make his point, he pulled the beam of his light off us and put it on the semiautomatic pistol in his other hand. Thank God for stupid criminals. By the time he returned the beam to me, I had the Python in my right hand and he was on its business end.

"Shit," he whispered. I couldn't see his face, only a flashlight beam. I went through the usual commands, so the suspect has no doubt what you're saying, and my nerve returned. I decided I would fire first directly at the light, then a pattern around it, just in case he were smart enough to hold it away from his body. So far, smart was not his MO. I decided I would give him five seconds to comply and then squeeze the trigger.

Something buzzed in the ceiling and a bank of overhead fluorescent lights came on. I nearly shot right then, but I hesitated. Then everything was clear. Malkin was standing ten feet away, his flashlight suddenly impotent. Lindsey was still beside me, now in a combat stance. Dana was here, too. She was standing nearer to us, beside an electric panel and some boxes. Now her hands were holding a shotgun. This was no hunting gun, either. It lacked a stock, and was made for close-quarters use by the police, or the bad guys.

"David," she said, "you are such a disappointment."

"Put your weapons down slowly, now," Lindsey said, shifting her stance toward Dana.

"Shut the fuck up, bitch," Dana said, and rather expertly worked the shotgun's slide action to chamber a round.

"Dana." This from Malkin. "Dana, we can't do this. It's gone too far already."

"Don't you get weak now, you son of a bitch," she hissed. "It's way too late for that. We wouldn't even be here if you hadn't been afraid that the body had been found. Your fear made that happen, Jerry. But we can fix it. They don't know anything."

"They knew enough to come here!"

"They don't know anything, baby." Dana's voice became reassuring, motherly. "So I was wrong about Mapstone being too stupid to catch on. But I also had the gut feeling we'd better come back in through the side door and make sure we hadn't been followed. It's going to be fine, baby. Nobody will figure this out. It's too complicated. We made it that way. So when they're dead, it's all tied up."

"You said that the last time," Malkin said.

We were in a mess, inside an isolated warehouse, in a Mexican standoff. Part of my mind wondered whether that was a politically incorrect term now. I tried to weigh the chances we had against the shotgun if all hell broke loose, and they didn't look good. I could fight fear and panic. Worry about Lindsey was harder. That's why married cops aren't partners. I tried to keep them talking.

I said, "It won't work, Dana. You'll have to kill a lot more people. We know from Jack Fife that it was you who wanted to hire serious muscle to intimidate Louie Bell into selling. That's how you got Adam Perez. And then you sent him to my office to kill your husband and me, and make it look like I murdered your husband and then turned the gun on myself."

Dana's mouth came open.

"That's right," I said. "Perez isn't dead. We withheld that from the media. And he's talking. He wants to avoid the death penalty. It won't be easy."

"David…" she began in a softer voice that chilled me.

I shouted her down: "Why did you have Perez kill Davey Crockett?"

"Who?" Malkin said.

"The cripple in the old school bus," she snarled.

He said, "Oh, my God, what have…"

"Shut up!" she screamed, and waved the barrel of the shotgun. Her finger was inside the trigger guard. There she was, my soccer mom, the non-student who had a non-crush on me, holding that shotgun with the same natural aplomb as Patty Hearst turned Tanya the Symbionese Liberation Army girl. She said, "We had to get those papers back! He was hiding them for Bell. Adam asked nice, and then he didn't ask nice."

Lindsey asked, "Was it the same for Alan Cordesman and Louie Bell?"

"Something like that," she mumbled.

Lindsey said, "It seems like a hell of a price to pay for a parcel of land…"

"You have no idea," Dana said.

Just then, Malkin put his pistol on the concrete floor. "I can't do this," he said. "Dana, it has to stop now."

She almost swung the gun in his direction, but kept it on us. She said, "Shut up, Jerry!"

"We can't kill two cops!"

"Baby, we're about to get everything we wanted!" she said. "Arizona Dreams, the water it has to have…"

I swallowed hard and said, "So that's it."

"So that's it," Dana said.

"How could you ever think you could get away with it?" Lindsey demanded.

"We will get away with it," Dana said coldly. She propped the shotgun on a box, keeping it trained on us. I had to settle for keeping the Python on her with aching arms.

I said, "Arizona Dreams never had enough water to meet the legal requirement of a one-hundred-year guaranteed supply. I bet the investors never knew that."

They just stared. I went on, "Alan Cordesman never knew that, at first. But the Bell property had the water, and you took it. Too bad it's not legal. The groundwater has to be on the property."

"That's the law now," she said. "The law will change. Among our investors are four state legislators. Arizona has to grow. That law is outdated. We'll build a pipeline from the Bell land."

"But you were certified as having a water supply at Arizona Dreams."

"Yeah, well," she said. "All that took was a crooked consulting hydrologist named Earl Rice. You met him back there in the water barrel. And then a lot of money for a man I know in the Department of Water Resources. Unlike Earl, he didn't get cold feet and threaten to betray us. The government is too overwhelmed by growth to pay much attention to every development anyway."

Lindsey said, "Do you really think you can hold two deputies at gunpoint here in this warehouse at Twenty-Seventh Avenue and Van Buren and not have anyone notice?"

"We won't be here long," Dana said. "Now drop your guns and get your hands in the air."

"You mean here in this huge white building?" Lindsey asked. "That's nine-nine-nine."

My neck tingled. Lindsey was giving the radio code for officer needs emergency assistance. I tightened my grip on the Python.

"Are you German or what, bitch?" Dana said. "Drop your guns!"

"That's not going to happen, Dana," I said.

She said, "I really thought you'd let this go, David."

"When I didn't, you sent Adam Perez to my office to kill your husband and me? The body count keeps going up, and you still can't tie it up."

"We wanted to be together," Malkin said, his hands in a pleading posture. "Tom lost his stake in Arizona Dreams. The gambling finally did him in. But it didn't matter, because Dana would be with me." He wiped sweat off his forehead. "How much, Deputies? Let's end this in a businesslike way. How much would it take?"

"Forget it, Jerry," Dana said. "These two are idealists. That's why they're broke. I was sure as hell not going to spend the rest of my life broke, or in debt married to a hypocritical politician. Arizona Dreams is going to change all that…"

"There's one thing I don't understand," I said. My voice was raspy. Saliva refused to come into my mouth, only to evaporate in the hot air. "Why would Adam Perez still be denying he killed Louie Bell and Alan Cordesman? And when I think about it, I agree. Beating and shooting are his style; not an ice pick." I looked at Dana. "I think that's more your style."

She just looked at me like an insolent teenager. "Too bad I can't get close enough to you, love." She surveyed me with the shotgun barrel. "It was really easy," she went on. "With Alan, his girlfriend was gone, and I rang the bell and asked if we could have a drink and talk. One thing led to another—he'd always been attracted to me—and later, when he was asleep, I just did it. Once you do it, it gets easier. So I found Louie in the casino. He wouldn't talk to me. He just ignored me and started playing the slot. And I came up behind him, and gave him a hug, and held him real close. He only shuddered for a few seconds when I put it in…"

The warehouse was silent except for a drip of water somewhere. It only fed my raging thirst.

"So why didn't you use an ice pick on your husband?" I asked. "Why trust Perez with the job?"

"For the children," she said evenly. "He is their father."

"Do not move!"

The sound made me jump a little, but then I felt salvation. This was a new voice, but I couldn't see where it came from at first. I kept the Python's dual sights on the middle of Dana's bilious orange blouse. Then I saw men in dark uniforms moving into the light. Jared Malkin raised his hands high into the air.

"All over, Dana," I said. "Don't be a fool."

She looked at me with something strange and cruel in her eyes, and then she blinked and lowered the shotgun. Instantly there were half a dozen Phoenix cops on top of her.

I looked at Lindsey. She smiled and indicated the small headset under her hair, and the cord running to her cell phone. "It's a good thing you're married to gadget girl," she said. "*Cherchez la femme*, right?"

Later, after I had consumed two cold bottles of water and Peralta had arrived, I walked over to the squad car and leaned down to the passenger window. Dana stared at me from behind the prisoner screen, her hair glowing dark red from the adjacent streetlights.

"Why me?" I asked. "Why pretend to be a former student? Why concoct the story about your late father's note?"

She stared straight ahead, and then said, "You're a dinosaur, Mapstone. There with your books and your history and your cases that nobody cares about. I heard enough from Tom to know if anything happened to you, nobody would care too much. The idea was to get Louie Bell out there, and make it look like he shot a trespasser, and then saw it was a deputy and killed himself. And we'd buy the land when it was all over."

"So what went wrong?"

"Bell never showed up. Perez got stuck in traffic on the 101." She smiled. "You just can't depend on people nowadays."

# Chapter Thirty-Nine

"There's going to be hell to pay," Peralta said.

No one disagreed. Lindsey, Robin, and I were arrayed around the kitchen on Cypress Street as the sheriff prepared his signature carnitas for dinner. The room smelled of garlic, onions, chili powder, and whatever mysterious ingredients went into his alchemy. Lindsey and I were nursing Beefeater martinis, while Peralta was on his second Gibson. Robin sipped white wine. Sinatra came from the stereo, overruling the sheriff's preference for country music or the Beach Boys. I half listened to "The Lady Is a Tramp."

"Hell to pay," Peralta repeated. "When it all shakes out, you're dealing with the biggest scandal in Arizona since Charlie Keating and the savings and loan blowup. Maybe even worse. We arrested a guy at the Department of Water Resources today. Malkin had paid him half a million dollars and secret shares in Arizona Dreams LLC to falsify the water certificate. We're looking at other departments in the state and county. How this development got approved is beyond me. Hell, there may be more like this out there. It may take months to find all the limited partnerships where assets were stashed. More cumin, Lindsey."

"It won't be the first time speculators tried to dupe innocent Easterners," I said. "It was common in the nineteenth century to promise land that was fertile and well-watered. People got to the West and found the land they bought was really nothing but desert."

"I knew you were going to try to teach, professor," Peralta said.

"I have a captive audience." I toasted him with my martini. "Tales of the water rustlers."

"What about Enron?" Robin said. "This was kind of like Enron with land and water, all smoke and mirrors and crooked accounting."

"It'll take years to sort it out," Peralta said. "Arizona Dreams is in bankruptcy court, and the creditors will end up owning land that's worth a lot less than they thought. Nobody will be building forty thousand houses there."

"Thank God," I said. "What about Tom Earley?"

"That'll come," Peralta said, sampling loudly from a wooden spoon. "He claims he's a victim—that Dana lied to him about Arizona Dreams, persuaded him to buy out the Bell brothers. She did all the bad stuff. He wants to testify against her. Give it time. The county attorney will take it to a grand jury. In the meantime, Earley's resigned. He's been repudiated by the Republican Party. Everybody who was his buddy last week has a knife out for him now. Suddenly the sheriff's office is the favorite department of the county supervisors. So I guess we'll just have to keep you employed, Mapstone. Hell, I'm even going to give you two love birds a vacation in October to take your train trip through the Rockies."

"I hear the manuscript of the book is finished," Lindsey said, rubbing my shoulder with a free hand. "And the title is, History Shamus?"

"I'm going to let the sheriff decide," I said. "When he finishes reading it, and micromanaging."

Robin said, "I think you ought to call it just that: 'History Shamus.'"

Peralta grimaced and took a pull on his Gibson. "All right," he said. "Let's do it." He looked at Robin with mock sternness. "And you, whatever your name is, you could have ended up in a shitload of trouble…"

"It's Robin Bryson," she said in mock indignation. "That was my dad's name. Lindsey Faith can vouch for it. The other name, well, I was married for a year. It didn't work out. That's a story for another time."

"We have time to listen," Lindsey said, giving an ironic smile. "Anyway, I'm glad you're going to rent the garage apartment here, even if you're a pain in the butt sometimes. Your escape from the jaws of the criminal justice system certainly ruined Kate Vare's day. Why doesn't Kate like you, Dave?"

"I'm getting hungry," I said.

"Patience," the sheriff intoned. "Mexican food is serious business." He was chopping vegetables, looming over the cutting board like a fairytale giant.

Lindsey said, "I'm just amazed that Jared Malkin thought he could get away with it. The water fraud would have been discovered sooner or later."

"Probably," Peralta said, wielding a kitchen knife. "But the idea was never to build Arizona Dreams. It was to cash in on the housing mania. Anybody building housing here can get money. All Malkin had to do was convince investors he had land with a hundred-year supply of water. He scammed some of the biggest banks and real estate investment trusts in the country, and some of the biggest homebuilders. He didn't care. By the time the roof fell in, he'd be long gone. At least that's what he hoped."

Peralta was transferring the shredded beef into Lindsey's largest All-Clad saucepan. I tried to grab a piece, but he threatened me with the knife in a very convincing manner. He handed a piece to Robin, then Lindsey.

"To die for," Robin pronounced.

Luckily, it hadn't come to that. Things were getting back to normal in Maricopa County. It was the usual run of summer mayhem: dead immigrants in the desert, suburban bank robberies, meth lab busts, and children drowning in green swimming pools. Enough villainy and heartbreak for any place. Things were getting back to normal on Cypress Street, too. I sat back and watched the scene in our kitchen. There were ghosts, of course: Grandmother preparing bacon for breakfast; Grandfather reading his newspaper, and a boy who grew into me. We Americans have become so disconnected from our dead. I would have been no different if I hadn't come back home.

Now, Peralta was being his lordly self. He was one of two people left in my life who had actually known Grandmother and Grandfather. Sharon Peralta was the other. I would never stop missing Sharon, but she had moved on and was happy. How could I deny her that? Friends come and go, and if you're lucky you can hang on, even at a distance. The next time Lindsey and I visited San Francisco, we could count on seeing Sharon, and a friendship universe would be even wider. I still didn't know if I could view Robin as a friend. But she was here and she was making a heroic effort to tamp down her drama queen moods.

She took Lindsey and me out to Paradise Valley last week, where we met her wealthy employer. So at least part of her story was real. I watched her cock her head and saw some of Lindsey in her. Somehow, it mattered to Lindsey to keep this sisterly connection, with all its flaws and raw nerve endings. I saw Lindsey watching me, then Robin, and her expression was unreadable. When I took the two of them out, Lindsey would rib me about "my harem." In bed, she would quip about being territorial. Irony and humor were her defenses. She gently rebuffed my efforts to talk about those weeks when she was away. And no part of me wanted to admit that for a few inebriated minutes one night I had been tempted by Robin. I had my own questions and insecurities, too. If Lindsey had been a teenage mother, would I love her any less? But if it were a secret that excluded me, one I didn't intend to probe, then would it be an itch I couldn't scratch? All this would take time. Sinatra sang "I've Got You Under My Skin."

"Mapstone," Peralta said, "what the hell are you doing?"

"Drinking and fiddling."

"What is that?"

I held out the wooden carving in my hand. "It's one of Lindsey's matruska dolls. There's a smaller doll inside this one, see, and a smaller one inside that, and so on." I disassembled it for him. "It's like the Arizona Dreams scam. A double-cross concealed inside a double-cross…"

Lindsey said, "Makes me wonder if we found all of them."

"Well quit being a liberal academic parasite," Peralta said. "Get the tortillas out of the oven. We're ready to start serving."

Later, we sat in the living room and talked more about the case. Peralta puffed happily on a Cuban Cohiba, sharing it with Robin. She lolled against him, and he didn't complain. He said, "It would be nice to think this would make the entire state take a deep breath and slow down and stop being so greedy." He watched a plume of blue smoke rise in the high ceiling. "But it won't."

"Someday soon the real estate bubble will burst," I said.

He contemplated the cigar. "Maybe that will be for the best."

# Epilogue

In December, the healing rains came. It rained so many days that people started to say the drought was over. The experts assured them that it wasn't, but that didn't stop talk of dropping conservation measures—even of revising the groundwater act. Lindsey and I talked about this as we drove out to Paradise Valley to a private art show. It was curated by Robin, and her billionaire had invited a hundred or so of his closest friends. Parking was no problem: valets were waiting to take my keys and escort Lindsey inside under an umbrella. She still looked great in a little black dress, and her hair glistened darkly. The weather was cool enough for me to wear a suit and one of the Ben Silver ties Lindsey had given me for my birthday. Under the portico, she took my arm and we went in to meet the swells.

Aside from the collections of Social Realism paintings, Depression-era posters, and photography, and several Frida Kahlos, everyone was talking about the wine cellar. It was bored deep into the side of Mummy Mountain. By the time I got to it, however, I was alone. The rain had stopped and the other guests were out on the vast terrace, admiring the negative-edge pool and the views of the billion city lights. Lindsey and Robin were talking to the billionaire in his study. I carried my martini and went into the mountain. It was a grand affair, with a fifteen-foot ceiling and more bottles than the wine department at the Central Avenue A.J.'s, carefully stored and catalogued. It was like a NORAD bunker for wine, guaranteeing it would survive apocalypse. The rough edges of rock were prominent on all sides. I was running a finger along a sharp granite edge when someone called my name.

"Isn't this delightful," said Bobby Hamid. I turned to see him leaning casually against a stainless steel and glass refrigerator. "I want one."

"I would have suspected you already had one."

He toasted me with a glass of wine, the liquid glowing like blood in the tasteful lighting. In his black suit, black shirt and shimmering dark blue tie, he looked like he had just stepped out of a Hugo Boss advertisement.

"I hope the holidays are good for you and Miss Lindsey," he said. "And the charming Miss Robin."

"You're lucky the sheriff hasn't arrived yet," I said.

He made his clucking sound. "I have no fear of the sheriff," he said. "Although not all our elected officials are so trustworthy. That unfortunate Tom Earley comes to mind, and his Lady Macbeth, Dana."

"I suppose."

"You are quite the hero," he went on, "bringing them to justice. You know, Dr. Mapstone, it surprises me that you would prefer a martini to fine wine."

"It's just a character flaw," I said, wanting to sidle toward the door.

"So much history in wine," he said, taking a dainty sip. "Ancient Persia was renowned for its wine, you know. And this collection! For the gods!"

He walked closer. "You and I, we have so many connections. I do savor them, rather like I savor this 1984 cabernet."

"I try not to dwell on them."

"David," he said. "I wanted to thank you. For Arizona Dreams."

I put the glass down as slowly as if it were nitroglycerine. "What are you talking about?"

"It will be in the papers tomorrow," he said. "I made an offer to the creditors, and it's been approved by the bankruptcy court.

Nobody has an interest in this being dragged on forever, not the least some very prominent Arizonans who were involved as investors. Some of them are out there on the terrace tonight. You remember how I said things just seem to happen in Phoenix, and nobody ever knows quite why."

"There's no water, Bobby," I said. "It's worthless desert."

"That may be, Dr. Mapstone," he said. "But it may not always be. Mr. Malkin was a con man, a—what is that fabulous term?—a grifter. But he also knew the way Arizona works. So I can be patient, and the creditors can get at least a few pennies on the dollar. And someday, when the time is right, the water rules will be changed and who knows how valuable the land will be?"

"I didn't realize you were into land speculation, Bobby."

"It's just a little subsidiary of my interests," he said, his eyes glittering. "The headquarters is actually at my office in Malibu. I call it Tonopah Trinity LLC."

Suddenly I felt as if half of each lung had collapsed.

"You." It was all I could say.

He smiled, his perfect dental work surreally white against his swarthy skin.

"You bought the Bell property."

"They were unfortunately behind in their taxes," he said. "I paid them, and acquired the parcel."

"And this mysterious sugar daddy in Malibu that Jared Malkin kept talking about…"

"Do you know he was once a star of pornographic cinema?" Bobby said.

I shook my head. "You. I should have known. With a body count like this, I should have known."

The smile disappeared. "I killed no one," he said. "I let them do that for me. I think Dana would have eventually killed her lover Jared. A nasty little woman, if I may say. Adam Perez was a useful strong arm with a taste for sadism."

"Bobby Hamid's game," I said. "And we're all just players. The kid in the school bus was a player, too, right? I should have known that beating was the signature Bobby Hamid treatment."

"Now, Dr. Mapstone, let's not be rash."

"Rash?" Now I closed the distance between us. I wasn't shouting, but my voice sounded foreign to me. "Rash?"

"Don't forget that I saved your life, David." He stared at me with eyes that were as black and dead as obsidian.

"That doesn't matter," I said. "You don't have a checking account with me. You're just a killer. And someday…"

"Are you threatening me, Dr. Mapstone?"

"Yeah." I pushed past him.

"Dr. Mapstone," he said sharply. I turned at the door and faced him.

"You misjudge me," he said, swirling the red liquid in his glass. "I don't intend to build houses on the Bell land."

"I don't care."

"Do you know what's under the Bell land? The aquifer is actually quite deep, and before you get to it, you will find one of the most magnificent living caves in the world. It will put Kartchner Caverns to shame. This is the truth, David. The Bell brothers found it, and told no one. I…well, I came upon this information, and hired someone discreet to confirm the cavern's existence. When it's fully explored, it will be a wonder of the world."

"There's just one problem with your role," I said. "You're a killer."

"I will give it to the state," he said. "I won't sell it. I will give it. All I ask is some recognition. Bobby Hamid Caverns State Park. I like that. Of course, I would keep the rights to the aquifer. In any event, my children can walk with their heads high. My family will be recognized as they should be. Make no little plans, Dr. Mapstone. They have no magic to stir men's souls. Daniel Burnham said that."

I said, "You're still a killer."

He looked at me for a long time, and finally gave a tiny smile. Then the wine glass shattered in his hand.